High DRAMA
IN
Fabulous TOLEDO

High DRAMA
IN
Fabulous TOLEDO

a novel by Lily James

FC2
Normal/Tallahassee

Published by FC2 with support provided by Florida State University, the Unit for Contemporary Literature of the Department of English at Illinois State University, the Illinois Arts Council, and the Florida Arts Council

Address all inquiries to: Fiction Collective Two, Florida State University, c/o English Department, Tallahassee, FL 32306-1580

ISBN: Paper, 1-57366-094-9

Library of Congress Cataloging-in Publication Data
James, Lily.
  High drama in fabulous Toledo / by Lily James.-- 1st ed.
     p. cm.
  ISBN 1-57366-094-9
  1. Toledo (Ohio)--Fiction. 2. Young women--Fiction. 3. Kidnapping--Fiction. I. Title.
  PS3560.A387 H54 2001
  813'.54--dc21
                             00-012513

Cover Design: Polly Kanevsky
Book Design: Ruixin Wang and Tara Reeser

Produced and printed in the United States of America
Printed on recycled paper with soy ink

This program is partially supported by a grant from the Illinois Arts Council

Acknowledgements

The author wishes to thank her husband, Joshilyn Jackson, Susannah Breslin, and Cris Mazza. Also the December mothers, the Bingo girls, the novelists at UIC, Jacques de Spoelberch, Fred Willard, and R.M. Berry. This book has benefited enormously from the input of many great brains.

for Martin

Contents

Chapter One

There was this really pretty girl named Ellen, who was engaged to be married to an implacable man named Martin. They lived together, and had regular schedules and habits, and progressed along toward the marriage at a steady pace that no one could criticize. Martin owned a bar. Ellen hung out there. Martin cleaned the bathroom. Ellen cleaned the kitchen. All the time, in the mind of Ellen, Martin had everything under control, and Ellen didn't.

Life is like a long cafeteria line, she thought. You choose one salad, rejecting all the others. You choose one vegetable, one meat, or a pasta side, and you choose a dessert, a drink, and that is that. Some sad people seem to choose the thing they want the least, because that is at least certain. Others linger on the choice, deliberating carefully between the chicken and the fish. Others seem to know exactly what will taste the best, floating along, gracefully selecting and consuming, out of ignorance or wisdom, what is right. Ellen liked to think that she had walked the line with eyes closed, and now stood in front of the cash register, staring at her tray, and it was all foreign, all decided by whim, nothing considered, but all uncontrolled, hasty, final.

She walked around the house with her engagement ring in her mouth, emptying ashtrays and garbage cans. She let the ring slide under her tongue, and then flipped it up to the roof of her mouth, moved her tongue back and back until the ring was almost down her throat. When she was a teenager, she had ridden her horse across a railway trestle over a river, a tributary of the mighty Allegheny, which is itself a tributary of the mighty Ohio, which is itself a tributary of the mighty Mississippi. It was a very dangerous trip, because the trestle was not a bridge. It was a trestle. This meant that the horse had to step carefully on each railroad tie. Nothing was below them but river and rail. She always set the reins down on his neck and put her face into his mane, letting him make his own decisions. She did this because she imagined that if she sat up to steer, she would be tempted to jerk his head to one direction, jab her foot into him, and send them both into the river, just to have the choice over with. This fall might prompt a daring rescue. Then she, changed by the experience, would probably make bold life decisions. Then would come the aggressive behavior, which would appear to her family strange but understandable. The ultimate move to Brazil or France, and the vast and unpunishable adventures that would necessarily follow, all this she had avoided by letting the sensible horse make his own way over the river. After all, it could have ended in only a bump on the head and wet clothes, fifteen miles from home.

She thought, What if there is no longer any time in which to reinvent myself? Maybe she could no longer become the kind of girl who just commands a room. She had already met everyone she would ever know, and she had already acted in a certain way: in a way that allowed her to be eclipsed. She had never imagined herself turning out like this, because she always thought that she could move away, or become famous, and her entire personality could change. Now it seemed like that would never happen, because there would always be Martin, and Martin would always know. Maybe, if she were to swallow her engagement ring, she could work very hard, become a dancer, or a painter, meet a whole new crowd, tour in many cities. She choked on it briefly, and spat it out. There were many moments in her life she had passed right through, ignoring every fork, forging ahead toward this, when everything could have been different, had she just veered suddenly left or right, or vaulted straight up. She put the ring back on her finger.

Ellen pulled on her t-shirt, letting her hand slide down over her long torso, feeling where the ring would be if she swallowed it into her stomach. She was long and smooth, with a long rib cage, and a greyhound neck. The room was really Martin's room, because he liked dark wood, and the burgundy and hunter green in the painting and the bedspread were his colors, not hers. She would have liked the walls bare. She would have liked to open the window, but it was caulked shut. She pulled on her panties. She always slept with panties on, white nighttime panties that came up to her waist. Her hair hung down around her face, falling on her shoulder blades as they stuck out of the t-shirt's stretched collar. If she had swallowed her ring, then that night when Martin came home, he would be untying his shoes, correctly, sitting on the seat of her vanity. When he had untied them he would pull them off and place them on the floor of his closet, where there was now just enough empty space in the row of shoes for the missing pair. Then he would stand up and pull his shirt off.

"I swallowed my ring," she would say. "It's in my stomach."

She thought that he would not be able to argue with this, that he would not be able to rectify it, adapt to it, assimilate it, or reverse it. But he might come over to her and bend her backwards over the foot of the bed, so that her feet were still on the floor and her upper body stretched across the sheets. He might place his hands over her sternum and move them slowly down until his fingertips butted against the bottom of her rib cage. It would be as if his skin were oiled, and hers made of silky wax. The way he slid over her, exhibiting almost professional sensitivity. Her hands would grasp the fitted sheet, which was well anchored, and could be safely tugged upon. Under her rib cage, his fingers would move on their own, deftly locating her stomach, causing her no pain. He would softly squeeze it, milking the organ slowly. Her torso would melt into a buttery pool of good will under his imagined attentions, and he would easily manage to ascertain to his own satisfaction that she had not in fact swallowed her ring. That she had made it up. Then Martin would withdraw his hands from her, and she would be saved.

"I think," shirtless Martin would say, standing back, "that if you do swallow your ring, you will be just fine. You will continue as you always have."

Martin, she felt sure, had never felt like boiling off his skin and inserting himself into a new life. Martin was the cold silent certainty behind every decision, the thing she could bounce back to after almost breaking off, almost leaping out over this or that imagined chasm, then pulling herself back breathlessly, refreshed. Martin had that helpful quality. If he was unimaginative, he was stable. If he was dry, he was clean. And under all of Ellen's erratic imaginings was this rock of Martin. Listening to her stereo with the right speaker unplugged she could hear strange versions of her favorite songs, with the backup singers too loud, and almost no snare. But there would always be Martin. It afforded her the luxury of her invented anguish.

The phone rang. She answered it, slouching over the small table in the hallway, pulling on her shoes. It was four o'clock. In fifteen minutes she would meet Martin for an early supper at the bar before it opened. This was every afternoon's plan, with martinis. In the phone against her ear, a man's voice on the other end said, "Can you hear me? Can you hear me?" When she said, "Yes," this man told her that he would be out in front of her place in five minutes. She said slowly, "Alright, I'll be there," and even though the voice then said, "I love you, Erika," she still went out front, and waited, for nearly an hour, for him to come, and pick her up, and take her away, believing somehow that if he could mistake the number, he could then mistake the address. Of course, he did not. It was a wrong number.

There was this difficult man Martin who was a hard worker and a water drinker. All his life he had been changing, and growing, and making himself into this person who was considerate, and dutiful. And he knew that he was going to marry Ellen, who was beautiful and smart. Martin made money for Ellen, and for himself, every day in his bar where he made a success happen. The bar was called "The Joyride," in memory of nothing that had ever happened to Martin. At one point in his life, Martin had been angry and alone. Now Ellen and Martin were perfect. It was a beautiful moment—much to be desired and nothing held back. It had seemed to Martin many times that he would not reach this possibility, but now here he was, at the top of his life, looking out on it.

Life is like a channel full of rough water that not only flows but rises, he thought. And you have to swim, up and fast, mechanically bending arms and legs in an established pattern once, again, again, again. And you swim up and up, strong and true, for a long time but not forever. The trick is to get to the topmost point of the channel, where the water meets the lip of it and it begins to spill, before you have to rest. Then you can enjoy one tiny moment of triumph, as you can see out over the edge of it, and see what is there, on the brink, on either shoreline. When you rest you float, and when you float you might as well be dead. Because you are a repugnant floating person. Martin knew in his heart that everything would have to slow down and stop, because bars and marriages don't last forever. In fact they don't last very long in a town like Toledo, which isn't even a college town, isn't even a factory town, just sits on the river swallowing things up.

It would all succumb to a slow rot, everything he had done, everything he had made, all the works of his hands and the perfection of his heart, because he was tired and anyway it was bleeding away from him, beyond his control. And as he looked out on either side of the channel he saw Ellen on one side and The Joyride on the other, and he felt that he would have to stop swimming pretty soon.

And then Martin had a vision, when he was silent and still, waiting with his hands folded for someone to come out of the men's room in the DMV. In the vision, Martin stood with feet twenty-four inches apart, arms clasped firmly behind his back, on top of the sign belonging to the grocery store across the street from his bar. His face blank, his muscles slack, his tall frame close to relaxed, he stood fully sixty feet above the sidewalk, feet planted. Martin stood on the grocery store sign, and waited for Ellen to turn the corner. She came on foot, traveling from their apartment to their place of employment, which was the bar that he owned.

When Ellen came around the corner, at exactly 4:15, arriving on time for the pre-shift early supper they always shared, he bent at the waist, leaned forward, and plummeted off the sign onto his head. As the vision panned back away from his body, he died quickly and mercifully of a severed spinal cord one fraction of a second after impact. Ellen ran across the parking lot, slapping her hands onto cars that got in her way. She zigzagged to him, fell on her knees beside him, and her lovely hair fell down on each side of her face as she leaned over him. He was crumpled, contorted, and she rolled him over, clasped his pallid cheeks between her palms, and searched his face for life. In misery, she wet his dead face with her tears as she sat astride him, pummeling his cold chest with her little fists. This is how the vision showed him that it would be. It was, in fact, very cinematic. In the vision he saw that, of course, he could become legendary, and Ellen could, and The Joyride could. Even in this stale and irritating city, people tell stories for years.

Of course, with him a suicide, they would all live forever. With him suicided so graphically and in the glare of day, there would be no denizen of Toledo who would not hear of him falling, of her finding, of the bar waiting there empty like a crypt out of which he would rise in the mouths of gossipers and the wheels of rumor mills and the lips of clubbers, punks, rockers, on the third day and into perpetuity. So he began a simple ritual, just to comfort himself, climbing up to stand on the sign and waiting for her to turn that corner.

On that day, with Ellen puttering around at home, Martin breathed deeply of the March air, wrapped his pea coat tight against the brisk wind and climbed to the top of the grocery store sign. At the very first glimpse of Ellen he would dive. And he thought that he would be glad to dive, because it was, after all, all becoming a failure. Just the other night, for example, several young men from the tattoo parlor next door had come into the bar, ripped the soap dispenser off the wall in the men's bathroom, and had kicked it around on the floor like a soccer ball, making a terrible mess. Stef, his bouncer, had come into Martin's office beet-faced and puffing with rage. Those tattoo boys had never made trouble before. And yet here they were kicking soap dispensers around in the men's john. Martin had had to speak to them out on the street, had forced them to go home, had made Stef clean up the mess. It was unstoppable, this creeping decay, these tired arms.

Martin remembered from his military youth something called ironically "The Bar." This was a long metal pipe rising perhaps 2.5 feet above the tile floor in a hallway between the locker room and the pool. New sailors had been made to straddle this bar, and run along it, sans underwear, to cleanse their butts and balls before entering the pool. In this dank, bright corridor, cold water sprayed up briskly from the bar at short intervals, like a long, terrible bidet. In Martin's perfect world, every citizen would run such a gauntlet twice a day. It would be referred to bluntly as mandatory anal cleansing, but it would never be discussed. No one talks about tooth brushing after all, and no one considers it an imposition.

Martin considered himself lucky to have lived this long. He tried every day to be courteous, brave, and temperate. While he would have loved to force-march the tattoo boys to the nearest shower and scour them bloody, he let them go home without even cleaning up their own mess. While he had daily thoughts of forcing Ellen into full-body armor to correct her apathetic posture, he never acted on them, never even said, "Could you please stand up straight?" Instead he operated an establishment where people came nightly to get drunk, fall over each other, make false declarations, vomit, piss. It was enough of the penance, for him, enough of the gradual crawl. He was ready to be out of it, beyond it, past it. If this for him was the limit, then let it be the limit.

Often, Martin imagined the perfect place of work. Employees would enter in their spotless uniforms— blue coveralls and red caps over white t-shirts and bright black boots. The plant would be underground, and the air and water would be brutally filtered. Every machine would clink respectfully. Every fingernail would be clipped. There would be no wasted words, no misunderstandings, no going back over what had already been done. No rats or mice would get in. The product would be shipped on time, effortlessly, in neat yellow boxes. At the end of a long, white hallway smelling of bleach, his office would be cut into the earth in a perfect cube, and he would stand there, in the middle of it, without a desk or an attendant, feeling the seamlessness of the operation, breathing in and out.

The world would churn ahead forever and ever without friction, without energy loss, without entropy, just beautiful. But instead, in the end, someone had to jump off a grocery store sign and save the world, because there is entropy, and sin, and there is friction, and slouching, and someone has to put an end to it before it all crumbles into dust.

At 4:20 Martin sighed wearily. At 4:30 he began to climb down from the sign, finding the familiar footholds without thought, and dropped onto the concrete in a black humor. After 4:15 it was never feasible, irritatingly ruined, ruined, ruined. He jerked his head to the right and left, sharply cracking the joints and scowling. Arms behind his back still, he marched into the club, ready to break heads open on his sharp, deadly chin.

Ellen and Martin lived in glorious Toledo, in the throbbing heart of Northwest Ohio, when the eighties were turning into the nineties, when the Gulf War was about to blow, when Flock of Seagulls had to give up and play small clubs, when bi-levels were becoming bangs. It was a dark little city on a black water, prideful and weak, flaunting its zoo and its smug little university, when its skyscrapers stood like ghosts silent at night and its shipping port cranes and elevators hung monstrous in the afternoon. People from Toledo wanted to be people from somewhere else. But in the interim, there was much cheer.

The Joyride was a tight ship. Upon hiring new employees, Martin had their astrological charts done, so that he would know everything about them, and would be able to predict them, arrange them, save them. It was a bright, smart thing Martin did. For example, he had hired Stef, sullen Slavic bouncer, because born under Venus and Mars, Stef exhibited strong affinity for both romance and violence. These traits made him a most excellent bouncer, because inevitably, he understood things. He was sympathetic, and yet he had a terrible potential for rage so fierce and irrevocable that everyone knew he could suddenly turn sour and bust some serious ass. The days of the month in which Mars was closest to earth were marked with red crosshairs carefully drawn on the office calendar. In these days Stef was expected to feel especially warlike, and was advised not to engage in any conflicts. This is why the tattoo boys conflict had made an impression on Martin beyond the usual barroom drama. It was a bad day for Stef. It required particular monitoring.

When Martin entered The Joyride by the front door that afternoon, shivering a bit and stomping, Stef was already behind the bar, washing glasses with a vacant expression on his wide face. His dark eyes smoldered with a distant thought. His arms moved mechanically. Stef was short, thick, quick. Martin knew that the glasses were already clean, because he had washed them himself before closing last night. One by one, Stef took the glasses down off the counter, washed them, and replaced them dripping.

"I was thinking," he said, although he did not visibly notice Martin's presence, "that maybe we could start a little kitchen in the back. Nothing major, just like a little kitchen."

Martin moved to the bar and took a seat in front of Stef. Inside his head, he imagined a small cushion of air under each shoe as he walked so that he would never touch the ground. His footfalls would be absolutely silent. He would walk with his fingertips outstretched, always touching the perimeters of his personal space. He would never blink. The funny thing was that everyone else also pictured Martin this way, a sleek, well-groomed overlord. He reached behind the bar, blindly locating a pack of cigarettes and a lighter. He pulled one out, lit it, and drew on it slowly.

"See, that way, when you and Ellen have your dinners here, you could just eat from the kitchen. You wouldn't have to order food or bring in carry-out."

Martin blew smoke out in a directed column. He didn't like bringing food in or ordering it in, didn't like eating in restaurants at all. He liked to wash his own vegetables, cut his own meat. But for the sake of convenience, he had given up his wild notions. He half-smiled at the fact that Stef had recognized this and was now bargaining with it.

"And then we could have like a short menu, you know, for the bar. Just appetizers. And I know someone who would come to work as a cook. Or Ellen, you know, needs a job."

"Ellen doesn't cook," said Martin, squinting.

"Well okay," Stef went on, accelerating his glass-washing, "I know this girl who could cook here, or work here."

In the four years that Stef had worked with Martin at his bar, he had never brought a friend to work, or a girlfriend. He had come alone to the Christmas parties that Ellen orchestrated, leaving early. Martin deeply, fully appreciated this kind of tight-lipped dispassionate behavior. But he couldn't help feeling a spark of curiosity as Stef now appeared to be asking for a job for a girlfriend. "No," said Martin. "No kitchen. Ellen's never on time for dinner anyway. We never have it."

"Fine, okay, I just imagined, you know, you could have whatever you wanted every day, and you could, you know, sit at a table with plates," Stef said, abruptly tossing his dishrag onto the faucet and backing away from the sink. Martin listened, but since Stef didn't press the issue, didn't ask for a different job for this girlfriend, Martin let it drop. For a while he imagined the bar as it would be in a few years when his death had become a myth. It's not like he expected air brushed pictures to appear on the wall with small lights attached to their frames. But a certain reverence would probably be appropriate.

By the time Ellen arrived, the bar was full. Ellen was supposed to be the hostess, a role she had imagined herself, thinking of pitchers filled with specialty drinks, casual greetings to regular guests, connections, knowing everybody, flashing smiles, glowing. But in this real life she was shy. There was a bubbling persona somewhere inside her, ready to blaze across the room and attract everyone. She put off bringing it out every night, until she forced herself to know that everyone saw her as quiet. She then revised this idealized self to be behind the scenes, thinking and moving and planning, being the classy demure proprietress, holding the strings, keeping out of sight, so that everyone would say, "I never knew!" or "Ellen? Ellen did this?" and gaze at her with new respect.

She watched the band for a while, and it was not a good band. None of the members had any stage presence. The stage stretched across the front of the room, next to the door, so that the window behind the band looked out onto the street. The bar stretched down one long wall, so that one end was close to the stage, and one end was far. In the back of the room was the sound guy. Behind the bar and a wall was a large room where bands could hang out, or store their equipment before they went on stage. Martin booked at least two bands a night. Once, Flock of Seagulls had played there. Lots of times The Connells did. Stef helped the bands load in and out, using a door to the back room, accessible from an alley. Ellen believed and had long stated that the bar needed to be completely redecorated. She thought this would be a good job for her.

She didn't like the stiff black stools, or the shiny bar surfaces. She didn't like the white walls and black and white tile, and she didn't like the bubbles in the tubes behind the bar. She thought it was trashy—too 1986. Perhaps she would draw up some plans for Martin, present them at his desk in his office, wear a suit, be praised. Perhaps she would oversee weeks of work while the bar was closed for redecorating, have hassles with workmen, enforce the contract, cry late at night with the frustration of it all, be comforted. Then when the bar reopened, she would nervously wear a new dress, and sit somewhere quiet and out of the way, to honestly judge people's reactions. Maybe someone would notice who would hire her to redecorate another bar. Maybe it would all fall into place, one thing after another, until she felt comfortable in Kenneth Cole pumps and a room full of men in wingtips.

She thought that a good idea for decorating would be to somehow mimic the natural light of afternoon. Martin called her a Protestant. Stef came over to where she was sitting at the bar and asked her if she was having a good time. This between them was code for "How are you?" Ellen started a conversation, saying mean things about the new waitress. Stef wasn't really listening. Ellen said that the new waitress was too quiet and uptight, and then said she was too outgoing and nosy, and when Stef agreed to both, Ellen decided to end the conversation.

"You're not listening," she said.

"Yes I am," he said truculently.

"You're NOT," she said, standing up. She looked through the dark bar for Martin, roving around with her eyes, and then slouching back down on the stool. Ellen asked Stef what he wanted to do that night, and he said that he wanted to do nothing, just nothing.

"I'm really not interested in doing anything," he said, and tapped his fingers on the bar. He was hunched over, one leg bent with its foot on the rung, one leg dangling. One shoulder hunched more than the other one. Ellen assessed him.

"Stef," she said, swinging her legs around petulantly, "How would you redecorate this bar, if you could? I mean if money was no obstacle?"

"What?" said Stef, jerking his head around toward her. "I have to go."

"Wait," Ellen pushed herself off of her stool and grabbed his elbow. "I want to go to the store and get some grape juice."

Stef eyed the floor, tapped his toe several times on the tile, and said, "No. Get Martin to take you later."

It seemed to her that Stef was her bodyguard. She liked to pretend that she was more than mildly pretty and moderately delicate. She liked to pretend that her glamour had to be shaded from the world by veils and gloves, that her companion was a bodyguard, not a coworker. When she walked, she tried to glide. When she knelt, she paid attention to her wrists, and the angle they made with her arms. She was, in her mind, always averting her gaze from the eye of some potential stalker, always slouching to conceal a hidden arch, smiling more slightly, gesturing more softly, always to keep a secret. If to the world this act appeared as simple fear, that was the world's mistake. Why did Stef really follow her around? He was Martin's employee, and Martin's logic was thick.

Later in the night, Martin came out from his office. Now the second band was playing, and they were better, louder. This was Martin's house band, Ten Pin, and they played here all the time, always bringing in their faithful following to poke their butts around and gyrate and laugh on the dance floor. There were always six or seven girls close to the stage who danced flawlessly through every set and knew all the words to the songs. Ellen still sat at the bar. She hadn't seen Martin since morning, and due to the wrong number episode, she had missed their little supper entirely. Martin wafted over to where Ellen was sitting, and picked up a martini glass. He placed into it three pieces of chipped ice, poured into it vodka, and then garnished it with three green olives. He placed it in front of her, keeping his eyes on the band, and around the bar.

"You call this a martini?" said Ellen mechanically.

"You call this a conversation?" he returned.

Ellen picked up an olive and sucked out the pimento. It was a drink she had "invented" called Olive Vehicle.

"I think we should commission a sculpture for downstairs," she said.

"Would you like to be the model?" asked Martin, now with his hands spread out on the sink behind the bar, his shoulders leaning forward heavily.

"Maybe I would," she said. "Maybe I would love to be a model."

"I didn't say 'a' model; I said 'the' model."

"Oh. Well in that case, no, I would not like to be 'the' model. I could never come in here again, after everyone had seen me naked."

"I wasn't thinking of a nude, actually," said Martin absently. "Where is Stef?"

"I asked him to drive me to 7-Eleven for a bottle of grape juice, but he wouldn't."

"Do you want me to drive you?"
"Can we go now?"

Chapter Two

Martin drove and Ellen rode in Martin's Buick to the 7-Eleven.

"If you didn't need cigarettes anyway, would you drive me?" she asked.

"I have cigarettes behind the bar, and I have cigarettes in my office."

"But you are going to go into the store and buy cigarettes anyway, right?"

"Yes."

She watched the lights and cars go by the passenger window, liked the feeling of being driven. She pushed her knees against the dashboard so she could rest her head against the window and just let Martin drive her. She could watch out the window at all the cheaper, dirtier bars, and all the buildings, the little clumps of people, the traffic signals, the river, going past under the telephone wires, flashing through her field of vision like a movie during the opening credits. In a car like this she could be anyone driving anywhere. They often made trips like this out into the night, to do this or that, run errands while the bar was open and in full swing. Martin said it was like watching the game from the stands—freeing and educational. Martin watched the other clubs' lines, their marquees, their parking lots, with academic interest. Toledo was not a city renowned for its nightlife, but that actually made the nightclub business more competitive. Ellen liked the contrast of the close, loud bar with the quiet car and the open sky. The city was a sprawl, an ugliness, but it was always cooler outside, and Ellen liked to think of herself positioned here, temporarily. Later she would probably say that she had spent a number of years in Toledo. At this "later" moment she would be in Bangkok or Hollywood, probably with a strange outfit on, probably on drugs.

"Why are you going to go in and buy cigarettes anyway?" she asked languidly, still letting her head drop against the window, feeling her hair get smashed on that side.

"I don't want to waste the trip," answered Martin, his face straight forward, his hands spread apart on the wheel exactly at ten and two o'clock, as he had been taught. He smiled tautly, lips barely moving.

Ellen sat up, and turned to him, her forehead wrinkled, her lips wet.

"You know," she said, gently turning after a moment and dropping herself back against the seat, "you are really an ass. Do you know that I can't wake you up at night even if I beat on you? Is that why you are marrying me? So someone will always be there to check and be sure you still have a pulse?"

Her face was twisted into a frown, but she was waving her arms around comically, signaling that she didn't even want to fight. Sometimes Martin was too dull and robotic even to engage in conversation.

"I drive you places so that I can go into the places for you and get you what you want," said Martin kindly, smiling at her, his eyes softly wrinkled just at the edges, "See? Good. Not bad."

He pulled into the 7-Eleven and parked the Buick.

"What if I want to go in?" she asked.

"Why should you have to go in? You want a bottle of grape juice, and anything else?"

"No."

He carefully tuned the radio to her favorite station, and left the car running so she could listen to it. He shut the door carefully, leaving it unlocked. Ellen leaned her head against her window again, listening to a song. Martin always went into the store, and always used his money to buy her things. This was so nice. He also always drove, when they were in a car, though there was talk of getting Ellen her own car, so she wouldn't have to walk the few blocks to the club every night. Sometimes Martin picked her up anyway, calling moments before she was supposed to walk out the door. Whether he did this out of a desire to save her the walk or out of a need for her to be there on time once in a while, she wasn't sure. She watched the people around the payphone outside the 7-Eleven, and wondered what they were talking about. What call was so important that it couldn't wait until they got home to make it? Why did people wait in line to use a payphone? Wouldn't it be easier to just go home? Or even to drive to the house of the person you were calling? Ellen didn't understand the urgency.

Once, before Martin had happened, she had used a payphone at the gas station around the corner from an ex-boyfriend's house. She had driven across town to his house, pounded on the door, and realized he was passed out. She had driven to the gas station, called him, and there was no answer. Then she had gotten back in the car, waited fifteen minutes. Back at his house again, she pounded on every window and door, screaming at him to wake up. She could not see into any of the windows, because he had stapled up sheets for curtains, and you couldn't pull them back, so he never did. After one last stop at the gas station payphone, where she left a tentative message about the next day, she drove back to her apartment and stayed there that night. She remembered thinking it was nice to stay in her apartment for a change, and that she would never again be so angry as when she was banging on his bedroom window, knowing he was in there. It made her glad that she had never slept with him. One of the best things about Martin was that he did not drink.

Ellen imagined herself standing at a payphone in Berlin, phoning Martin. She could not fully conceive of Berlin because she had never been there. But to her it was an international city. There would be long stone buildings, wet streets, dismal sidewalk traffic. It would be October. She would say, with her ear pressed tightly to the black receiver, eyes scanning the foreign words on the machine, that she needed to place an international call. It would be the middle of the night, almost morning, and she would have been out all night, carousing. She would tell the operator to ring The Joyride in Toledo. Martin would answer the phone in his office, and say, "Joyride, Martin" as she now said, "Joyride, Ellen" when she answered the phone. But she would be far away, in the dark, in a foreign country, alone. She would have friends, maybe journalists, but their companionship would seem empty to her, she would be tired of the glamour and the high life, yearn for him, and they would talk quietly and intimately until a cab full of friends arrived honking to whisk her off for more parties, more wine. She would say, "Goodbye Martin! I have to go!" and he would say, "Come home soon," and she would hang up, knowing that she simply could not now go home, nor could she ever go home, because she was a tragic cosmopolitan. Maybe she was a political prisoner, interned in hostile territory. Maybe she had committed a great crime.

The sound of the car door opening jutted into her reverie, and she didn't bother to turn her head as Martin slid heavily into the seat and closed the door hard behind him. Instead she put her hand over onto his sleeve, grasping his arm for just a second. The sleeve was thick wool, but she couldn't feel the arm beneath. There were layers of wool under her hand. This man was not Martin. The man tossed the gear shift up fast into reverse, stomped on the gas, then jerked it down into gear and peeled out of the 7-Eleven parking lot. Ellen jerked her hand away and cried out, "What—What—What are you doing?" She had to immediately believe that this was some kind of joke. The man beside her wore a huge thick pea coat, and more layers under that, snow pants, thick boots, a face mask and a hat. He was dressed for the Arctic. He did not look at her or speak, but accelerated onto the four-lane street, ran a red light, and Ellen realized slowly that she didn't know this man, that this was no joke, that a strange man had come into Martin's car and was now stealing it, with her inside. Ellen sat up on the seat facing him, bracing herself against the seat with one arm and against the dash with the other.

"Pull over!" she yelled at the man. "Stop!"

He didn't look at her or slow down. He made a turn, and headed for the freeway. Ellen turned to the passenger door and clutched at the handle, but the man clicked the automatic lock shut, and held his finger down on it. With his other hand, he deftly and tightly grabbed Ellen's left arm, gripping it so hard she cried out. He was steering with his knees, blowing through another stoplight, approaching the on-ramp to I-75 South. Ellen writhed in his grasp, hammering with her other arm on the door's window. Vainly she tried to roll the window down with a button—he had his finger on the up button as she was pushing down, then switched back to the door lock button before she could. He navigated bumpily onto the freeway, still using his knees to steer, and Ellen in a flash remembered her older brother as a teenager, dropping her off at elementary school while he worked a Rubick's Cube in his lap with both hands. As she had screamed at him then, she screamed at this man now, "Steer! Steer, or are you trying to kill us both!?"

She took her right hand off the instrument panel on the door and made a show of putting it in her lap. He put his left hand on the wheel and the car hurtled in and out of traffic faster now that he controlled it.

"Who are you? What are you doing?" she asked him, her voice a whine, for she was desperate. It was hurting her arm to have it gripped like that. If she could get the window down, she could get out. If she could get the child-lock off, she could get the window down. She would have to throw herself across the man's lap and jab at the button. It seemed so inconceivable. A moment ago, grape juice with Martin. Now, panic. Still he didn't move or speak to her. She thought that maybe he really was just stealing the car. That she happened to be inside, and on his agenda, her disposal was a subdirective. Maybe she would be thrown out of the car after they got outside town. This would be alright, she told herself, still feeling the pain of his fist around her left arm, but now sitting back against the seat, eyes wide open, madly thinking. She would roll down into the ditch, then come lurching back out of it covered in bits of grass and patches of dirt. She would be dizzy, having knocked her head on a rock. Then she'd stand at the side of the road, try to walk, and someone would pick her up and take her back to town, where she would fall into Martin's arms, taking time to graciously thank her roadside savior (as she would call him) and then get quite exhausted talking to the police and have to be carried home. She would spend a week in bed. Her captor sighed deeply, and settled into the fast lane doing about 85 miles per hour. There was no pursuit.

"Are you going to kill me?" she asked, "Where are you taking me? What do you want?"

When the man didn't move or speak, she swatted at his face with her free arm, drawing in a gulp of breath and thinking she would force him to acknowledge her. He was too terrible under all those clothes! She swatted at him three times, working herself up into a bit of hysteria, believing she would flail him, or throttle him, hook her thumb into his nostril and pinch, so he would beg her to let go. But he turned toward her menacingly, taking his eyes off the road to glare into her face from dark pits of eyes inside the mask holes. Ellen let her bravado turn to tears and dropped her face, smacking her knee ferociously with her other hand. Maybe he was going to torture her, kill her. Maybe she would only escape with her life and be raped forever, never able to sleep without nightmares, or permanently wounded. Maybe he would cut off her face, or her hands! Maybe he was an insane murdering killer! She sobbed freely into her lap now, thinking that she was not a brave brave girl, that things like this didn't happen to her, that she would fail, utterly, miserably, and be killed and end. She choked and cried, regretting every bad thing, every questionable motive. But maybe he would not kill her. Maybe he would torture her forever. Or sell her into a work camp, or to terrible foreigners. She could write a book about her experiences, sneak out the manuscript, and it would be published by a foreign press. Copies would be circulated through the American Underground, and Martin would come upon one, recognize her, come for her, find her.

She sat up in the car, wiped her tears, and recognized the landscape rushing by. They were going south on I-75. Soon they would pass Perrysburg, then Bowling Green. It was all real. As she sat there in the dark in the cold car with the sweating man in his overclothes, a realization crept into her mind, with mingled terror

33

and anticipation. This was no longer a contingency, or a dread, or a dream. Something was happening which would change her forever. In the middle of all her fear and her secret balking was a seed of determination, a tiny tingle of resolve, that this would not slip by. She could step to the watershed.

"Listen," she said to the man. "Tell me where you are taking me. What is going on? I have to know. Please tell me."

Her voice caught in the middle of her sentence as he braked suddenly, pulling the car off onto the median. He reached over with his left hand to put the car into park, never relaxing his grip on her. The man was strong. She would have bruises. He shifted in the driver's seat so that he was facing her, and his eyes held hers as she became frightened, trying to figure out if this was the moment, and what would happen, and if this was the end. Maybe she would die. Right now.

He struck her across the face with his left fist, hurting her nose and smashing her against the seat. Then as she crumpled he released her arm, lifting his right fist and bringing it down hard on her temple. She lost consciousness.

At the 7-Eleven, Martin tried to use the payphone, but there was a line.

Chapter Three

In the tunnel, it was all brightness. Ellen could not see the brightness because there was a cloth tied over her eyes. She was on the floor with her back to the cold tile, sitting on the cold floor. She thought that it was probably bright, because of the feeling in her eyes and on her hands. Her hands were tied. Her feet were also tied. She was not scared right now. She was physically miserable instead. She wanted a drink of water, or juice. She wanted to stretch out and lie down and go to sleep, but she thought she should stay awake in case he came back. She had been on the floor in the tunnel for a long time, she thought.

First, she had been passed out in Martin's car with the man. Then she had come to with the man shaking her. Her head hurt, but she thought that at least she was awake. Then he had pulled her out of the car and carried her over his shoulder to another car. He had put her down into the passenger seat of this car, and had knelt beside her, tying up her hands behind her back, and her feet very tightly, and putting the cloth over her eyes. She thought that the cloth was cotton. She thought it was white. The blood on her head had probably gotten onto the cloth, making her a gory figure, like a hostage or a prisoner of war. She smelled the new car only, did not really see it. It smelled nice, and she was sitting on leather. She still did not know what the man wanted to do with her, or if he had just wanted Martin's car, or what it meant if that were true. She thought that her disappearance might bring about news articles and interviews with Martin. Or did this sort of thing happen in Toledo every day, bringing almost no attention to itself?

She wasn't gagged. She could talk to him. She could ask him more questions, more questions about who he was and what he was doing with her. She thought she would ask him, "Who are you?" but possibly he would refuse to answer. She knew that if he didn't answer her she would be much more scared, so she had to think of a question that he would answer. A question he would have to answer, or that would surprise him into answering. She wished she had looked at him more before he tied and blindfolded her, to figure out what kind of person he was, and what he would respond to. But that was ridiculous.

"I'm scared," she said. He didn't answer. Maybe he was working for someone else. He was paid to take her, or maybe he just wasn't interested in her. She didn't talk any more because she couldn't stand it if he didn't talk back. It irritated her that she couldn't get him to talk, because it seemed essential to the general scene that he talk, or that she at least know at some point what was going on. But if he wouldn't talk, she couldn't keep pestering him. Maybe he had hit her because he was mad at her. Above all other things at that moment, she didn't want to be hit again. She had a blinding headache.

After they got into the new car, they had driven for a long time while her headache came and went, and she intermittently laid her head down on her knees, all hopes of escape gone, and then they went into what sounded like a parking garage. It sounded hollow and echoed. She remembered to remember all of this, thinking that she would call someone. The man had carried her down several flights of stairs, opening metal doors. Then he had put her down on the floor, and left her, walking away so she could hear his footsteps for quite a while before they died out.

She remembered when she was little on the farm where her father worked, and playing with the children of the other workers. They had a game called "Blind" where they would tie leg wraps around their heads and move around the farm slowly, crouching, mincing, feeling their way around for a certain amount of time. It was one person's job to keep time, and run about and be sure none of the blind people ran into any trouble. At the end of the decided amount of time, each person had to call out where they thought they were, what room, what pasture, and then rip off the blindfold and see if they were right. The only rule was that if you heard hoof beats coming, you had to drop to the ground, curl up very small, and wait for them to pass. In this way, they imagined they were staying out of harm's way. Ellen's father, who was a shit-shoveler, did not approve of the game. Whenever he found them playing it, he would hook his finger under the blindfold, and pull it down around their necks. This added an interesting dimension to the game. So, theoretically, she should have felt comfortable.

But she felt helpless with the cloth on her eyes. She felt like she couldn't fight or run, and that eventually the cloth would be taken off, and then she could. She didn't know how to move her legs when they were tied together. She didn't know how to use her hands when they were behind her. People in movies always seemed to manage it alright. Maybe he would come back before she had to try it. If she had worn something more lithesome, or if she had not worn a coat, she would not have felt so bound up. But she was glad of the coat, because of the cold. It was a schoolgirl coat, with a velvet collar, and hung to her knee. She wore black tights and loafers with a heel. She wore a skirt, and a blouse, and the blouse was white, and the skirt was black. It wasn't tucked in. Now maybe it would never be tucked in again. Sob, she thought with a wry smile.

An hour passed and she had not tried to untie herself. She thought about how she would explain all this to her grandchildren, how she would explain it to Martin. She started putting sentences to it, like "I was too dizzy to understand that he was tying me," sentences to explain her strange acquiescence. "I just had to know who was holding me captive" to explain her current excitement. Everyone would understand. There was a lot of fear in it, but also a lot of nervous anticipation. In a strange detached perspective which she liked, this was a great drama, and she was in the starring role. She thought this sentence several times: "I have never before been blindfolded against my will." She had not moved since she had been set down, on her butt, with her hands behind her. She had been sitting, waiting. She hadn't thought that it would take this long.

Ellen braced her feet against the floor and pushed herself up the wall until she was standing. Then she bent over, pulling her tied hands down over her butt until they were behind her knees, under her skirt. She rocked backward, bumping against the wall, and pulled each leg out through the circle of her tied arms. Now she could take the blindfold off. But she did not.

She knew that it was a bright room. She didn't really want to know how big it was. She knew it echoed when her heels tapped on the floor, but she didn't want to know how close the other wall was to her. It wasn't like playing Blind on the farm. She didn't want to explore; she wanted to sit, and be discovered, be claimed, be taken somewhere else by her kidnapper. She waited for him for more hours. She picked absently at the rope around her ankles. This would come off, she thought. She took it off. The rope fell away easily, with a little prodding at three knots. There would be no rope burns, no disfigurement, unless he retied her when he came again, and tighter this time. Maybe he would be in a fury that she had gotten loose. Maybe he would storm and rail at her, all in silence. Maybe he was a mute. Now she could walk, but she sat. More time. Now she had to go to the bathroom.

Abruptly, Ellen stood up, and with both fists clenched pushed the blindfold off her face. The tunnel was long and white, and bright. She looked both ways, up and down it. The blindfold, now on the floor, was white soft cotton, like a diaper, with a dark red stain on it from her blood. The bridge of her nose was bloody, she could feel with her hand. It was dried and swollen a bit from where he had hit her the first time. It was sore, but the headache was gone. Maybe he had given her a painkiller when she was unconscious, a powerful, merciful injection of painkiller so that the injury wouldn't bother her.

"I can walk," she said, and the words echoed down the long corridor, so she hollered "I can see!"

She ran down the corridor in one direction for a while, carrying her tied hands strangely in front of her, and since she didn't come to the end of it she ran back down it in the other direction. She came to a door, made out of metal, with a complicated handle like on a freezer.

"Come on! Come get me! Let's go!" she yelled at the door. She wondered if the man would be rough with her again. Why beat her up? Had she provoked it?

"How long are you going to leave me down here, you fucking bastard?" she roared at the door, hearing the sounds of it carry on behind her in the tunnel as echoes. She tried screaming as loud as she could, wondering if she had ever screamed this loud before in her life. Probably when she was less than two years old she screamed this loud, proportionately to her lung size at the time. When she was a teenager on the farm in Western Pennsylvania, she had screamed loudly on trail rides to chase away deer that might have been waiting in bushes to scare her horse. She had screamed, "No deer anywhere near!" In her adult life, she had never screamed at all, except at movies, in little bursts. Finally, she turned around and trotted all the way back down the tunnel to the other end, which was a white, plain wall made out of plaster. Knocking on the wall with her hands, she decided there must be brick or dirt behind it. Was she underground? She might be underground, underneath a parking garage, in a terribly clean tunnel designed for sterile storage. She sat down next to the white plaster wall and tried to figure out how long she could hold it without going to the bathroom. Probably for two hours. If she were on a car trip, and felt like this, she would be able to last for about 150 miles.

She waited for what she thought was two hours, pretending that she was riding in a car across the tundra of Alaska. She was riding in a car across the tundra in Alaska, and she was an old, old person. She was the kind of old person who understood when the ice was safe, who had once been stuck with a broken snowmobile over 100 miles from town, and had had to walk it back in, falling in the ice, warming herself with her hands, stripping down to nothing, rolling in the snow, almost going crazy from the lack of horizon, but saving herself with multiplication tables. She was the kind of old person whose eyes were wrinkled but didn't shut, and who had to be prodded in order to speak.

She would not be a person to sit by the fire and bore the young people of the town. She would not be a person whose stories were known by all, often repeated, until they were memorized by children, mutated, misunderstood, dismissed. In fact, she would almost never tell her stories. When she came to be 100 years old, and lay down finally, and died, she would have one remaining story to tell at the end, a story that no one had heard before, about things that no one ever knew had happened. It would be surprising, and then she would die, and everyone would marvel at her restraint, how she had managed to keep this from them for so many years.

She stopped thinking about this when she had to go to the bathroom so badly it hurt and itched and tickled. She decided that she would take down her skirt and tights and pee in the end of the tunnel by the white wall. But then, if he came for her while she was peeing, it would look stupid. Her tights would be down around her ankles and she would be propped against the wall trying to keep her shoes out of it. She waited, stretching herself out on her back on the floor to ease her bladder, and then eventually she got up and peed. He didn't come, or see her peeing.

In fact, eventually she had to pee again, and he had not come, nor had anything happened. Then nothing happened for a lot more time. She needed a drink of water, and a change of clothes, and a shower, and a bowl of soup, and a blanket, and to sleep. But she did not think she should go to sleep. She still thought she should stay awake, and wait for him, whoever he was. She remembered a parable about a lot of girls, and pots of oil, and some girls' lamps went out, and some girls' lamps didn't.

She propped her back against the metal door and put her forehead down against her knees. Maybe he would not come for her, ever. She was beginning to be a little lightheaded from hunger. Maybe she would die in this tunnel. She thought about how she would arrange herself for death, if she felt herself starving. If she felt herself starving, she would not claw at the door and scream herself hoarse, and die with a look of agony engraved on her features. She would lie down in the center of the floor, exactly halfway between the ends of the tunnel, and she would count the bricks down from each end, to be sure she was exactly centered. She would stretch out both arms and her legs as far as she could, as if trying to touch the walls of the tunnel. Then she would feel so very thin, and from fasting she would achieve a deliberate peace, and feel herself floating, and it would not be so very awful to die. Years and years later, excavators would come and dig up this tunnel, because it would have been underground, and they would find her entombed like a pharaoh in tile.

She thought that if he waited much longer, her hair would be miserably ruined. It would be greasy from not being washed for so many hours. It would be sagging from her crushing her head up against the wall. There would be a smashed in place in the back, like bed-head. She wanted to look as good as possible, for reasons she couldn't quite grasp. It seemed to her like a horror movie, where the heroine, though in dire straits, always manages to shine. Despite the nose wound, she might have glossy hair. A movie was her only real comparison for how she felt, and she did not want to have bed-head. It was a matter of knowing where you were, or setting to order those few things still under your control. She couldn't help thinking of herself as being seen by him, and she could not imagine what it would be like when he came in again. But she could also imagine a hundred things. He could be so different, from anything she had been used to, or he could be so awful, and hurt her, and kill her. She wished that the lights would go down low. She fell asleep.

When she woke up, she was very critically sincerely upset. She wanted a toothbrush and a face wash, and a drink of water. She started to cry with loneliness, and wished that she was back in her house, with Martin, and the stupid cat, and that she was planning what to wear to the club, and that she was making a little supper, and that it was something liquid, like chicken broth and wine in a skillet with little pork birds stuffed and simmering. She had seen Martin make pork birds. She thought that it was three o'clock the next day. She cried and cried, snuffling into her hands, which were stiff and ached from being tied. Missing Martin was terrible. He should be here with her. He shouldn't be somewhere else, leaving her here alone. Martin should come here and pick her up. Good Martin who was never involved in this kind of craziness because he just wouldn't be. He would be too busy doing right things. His arms should go around her and warm her, and make her feel good. These were her simplest thoughts. Still groggy, she fought off feelings of panic, where her thighs and shins tensed up, and she wanted to smack her head into the tile walls. Her eyes hurt from sleeping with the lights on. Her back hurt, and her hands hurt. She cried deep horrible sobs, coming up from her stomach, and she lay down on her side, letting her legs curl up, letting her head rest on the floor. She closed her eyes very tightly and just let herself cry and cry, for a long time, and then she lay there breathing.

"At least I can get these ties off my hands," she said, but the sound of her voice was very pathetic, and made her cry again because it sounded so alone. She was never going to get out of this tunnel! She was going to cry and cry, and then die, and it wouldn't be dramatic, or like a pharaoh at all. She would panic and scream at the end, and she would scratch at the door and beg, and her eyes would be dreadfully puffed up, and her hands would be swollen, and it would stink after she was dead. The entire tunnel would smell like rotten flesh, and it would be ugly when they found her, ugly with her body all stuck to her clothes. She thought she would have to wait a long time to die, and wished they would turn the lights down, so she could sleep during that time, instead of panic.

She sat up, thinking that one thing she could do was to get her coat off. The wool of it was irritating her wrists, and the velvet collar was irritating her face. She had never been in a coat for this long before. She had to get it off, immediately. Her coat could be used as a cover, or a pillow, after she'd gotten it off, and she could stretch her arms out. She worked at the knots around her hands, bending her wrists over and turning her fingers back to reach them. It was hard. At one point, she got very pissed off, and put her knee up through the circle of her arms, put her shoe down over the ties, and kicked viciously and hysterically, hurting herself. Fortunately, it was too awkward to kick very hard. Otherwise she might have ripped her hands off. When she thought of ripping her hands off she laughed, and then she felt stupid for crying. After a horrible breathless panic, if nothing dire happens, there is always a respite of practical calm. She worked quickly and got the ties off. She took her coat off and laid it down on the floor. For the first time she realized that there might be a surveillance camera in the tunnel. This thought made her feel bad, but then she thought that she could review her actions later, on tape, in a police office when everything was over and she was wrapped in a blanket, drinking tea. That would make her feel better. She might even be able to laugh.

Stretching in her blouse made her feel better too. Now she was all free. She liked her blouse. It was white and had a stiff collar and an open neck, and came down to points at the bottom. Of course just now it was wrinkled and smelled. Her skirt was a stiff little black number, which barely reached down to her knees, and her tights were thick for winter, but not fuzzy. She was tallish. She had a good, prominent bone structure and golden skin. Her nose was hurt but her body was working otherwise. It was possible she could live for a long time, or dig out, escape. She had to figure out what time it was, and when to sleep.

The door handle clicked and the door opened abruptly.

Chapter Four

Martin was concerned. He was away from his club on a busy night. His girlfriend had disappeared in his car. He had stepped into the gutter and collected a glob of vile jelly on his shoe. Not that Martin equated these three difficulties—he did not. But there it was. Sitting in the police station, the wet and dirty shoe seemed more real to him than the disappearance or even the abandoned club. It was all otherwise for Martin suddenly. The train had been derailed by this disturbing circumstance. He was sitting in a police station, which was unpleasant at best, and in his present state it was absolutely unnerving. Yet he sat at the police station waiting to file a missing person's report. A number of hours had to go by. He would let them go by, and then file it. This was simpler than going back to the club, going home, with Ellen nowhere, gone.

And in some way, he felt like it was his fault. It's not like Martin didn't understand blasphemy. Martin did. A person considering suicide understands blasphemy in a way that a person expecting a long life cannot. Did he not see that he was pretending a trinity, that he was pretending a messianic vision? That he, Martin, was planning to die, to become a martyr, to become a savior of Ellen and The Joyride, that through his death he would live forever, and all kinds of other blasphemous things that were only occurring to him as the vision became more permanent in his mind? Yes he did see. But Martin didn't want to be Jesus—the thought confused him. He had the same healthy respect for the Catholic church that he had for any institution with wealth, power, and a long history of oppression. But in his heart, he believed himself to be an atheist. His vision, he believed, was purely secular. After all, it might be a coincidence of messianic visions—how can you really have one that doesn't reference religion in some way? It was less blasphemy than plagiarism. Yet could it be that some angry god had avenged himself on innocent Ellen, only a supporting actor in the drama that he imagined, to prevent its taking place?

He had already reported the car as stolen, and had argued with the police officer about it. The policeman thought, naturally, that Ellen had taken the car. Martin thought not. The policeman was adamant. Kidnapping, he had said, was after all so very rare. It just didn't happen very often, and when it did, it was to rich people or criminals. Was Martin rich? Was Martin a criminal? Laughter. No, the girlfriend had taken the car. Still a pisser, but what can you do? Girls! Martin had distractedly agreed, having not considered the possibility of Ellen's betrayal.

"Some people don't show it when they're about to go off," the policeman had said. "They just go."

Martin considered the possibility that Ellen had run away with the car. But Ellen did not drive. Maybe she had taken driving lessons from Stef, in secret. Maybe she had been planning this for months, and already had a new place, a new name, a new identity, a new lover. But why would she take his car? Why wouldn't she just leave him? Ellen was a restless girl. Ellen was given to fits of impulsive thinking, but never before had this thinking materialized into action or escape. Maybe her disappearance was a cosmic intervention to stop him leaping from the sign and plunging the world into sanctimonious salvation. Or apocalypse. Or plunging himself right down to hell. Or maybe she had "gone off." If this was the case, however, he felt confident that Ellen would contact him within a few hours. She would not leave him to think that she had been kidnapped or hurt in any way. He was, in any case, her fiancé. She might even offer to walk around the corner of the grocery store and peel his remains off the sidewalk after he fell, pretending never to have left. In a purely non-Mary-Magdalene sort of way.

The police station downtown was mostly green and also wood. In the street, Martin had had trouble even getting a taxi, but here, papers were being signed, hallways traversed, tile floors tapped with black shiny shoes, drinking fountains used, drawers opened and closed, files pulled and replaced. Martin found it sleepily intriguing. However, underneath all the usual reserve, he felt a small kernel of fear. He did not want his life to be forcibly reshaped. He did not want a dramatic turn of events. No brave rescue, no mad escapades. He wanted to see her come through one of these windowed doors immediately, and then take her home, and undress her, and put her to bed. In the morning he would hear her popping microwave popcorn, and they would talk about it briefly. She always agonized over whether the popcorn was done, saying "one one thousand two one thousand" out loud between pops to judge when two seconds passed, and then saying "done" under her breath. They would talk about how whatever happened had happened, and then he would go to work and she would go shopping or job hunting or something. He did not want anything to be his fault, particularly the disappearance and demise of his one beloved.

He sat on a wooden bench, out of everyone's way. He felt excruciatingly tired, as if he had to go home and sleep, and then come back and worry, and do this thing he was doing, this brand new hateful thing. He went into the bathroom and peed, and looked at himself in the mirror, making his mouth flat and seeing his black combed hair. He thought that in the morning his eyes would go up at the corners, not down. In the morning his face would be scrubbed, not bristly. In Martin's line of work, he found it necessary to shave twice a day. He would have liked to shave immediately, there in the police station bathroom, before opening the door and looking out at the busy policemen. Instead he went back to the bench, but someone was sitting on it. She was a tiny policewoman. She sat with her legs open, but she was wearing pants, and a large black belt and no gun. She looked like she was about the same age as Martin but older than Ellen, which would make her exactly thirty.

She had red hair, curly, tucked into her policewoman hat. He imagined it was very long. If he had not been engaged to Ellen, and he had not been worried about Ellen, and he had been in a different universe where such things could have happened, she might have looked up at him and said, "Hey, do you want to go to my house and play some cops and robbers? I'll be the paragon of virtue and you be the errant knave. I'll force my morality onto your dire evil soul." He thought that this was the type of person that she was. He thought she would enjoy domination games, because she was a policewoman, and female. He walked over to the bench, but did not sit down, because she was sitting in the middle of it. She slouched back, knees out, weight flat on her tailbone, and glanced up at him with very big brown eyes. Her uniform was too big. Her body made angles in it. The hat, especially, was ridiculous.

She saw him, then looked up at him sharply, furrowing her brow, sitting up, "Are you the guy with the escaped girlfriend?"

"Yes," he said, as if speaking for the first time, abruptly formal, raising his eyebrows and moving his hands out in his pockets. "Actually yes, I am."

"Escaped from a 7-Eleven," she said.

"Yes."

"With your car."

"Well," he paused, feeling awkward, "it's a little complicated. I wouldn't want to tie you up."

He glanced around the room, appearing distracted, purposefully preoccupied. She flipped her hands out so that her little arms fell outstretched on the bench on each side of her body.

"I'm off duty," she said.

"Well then," said Martin kindly.

"But," she added, letting her eyes roll up to meet his, "I'm going to solve your case. I want to find this girl of yours and bring her back."

"There isn't even a case yet," he said. "I haven't even filed a report."

"I'm Jane," she said, sitting up and extending her hand. They shook hands and she kept hold of his hand, pulling him down. "Have a seat," she said.

He sat down, carefully folding his coat under his thighs, as was his habit. She let go of him and turned to face him, flipping her legs up onto the bench and folding them tightly, tucking each black shoe in behind her knees. Her back was perfectly erect now, and her head tipped attentively toward him. He imagined her hair falling down around her body. It would be unruly, crinkly in stiff red-headed crinkles. She would constantly tuck it behind her ears. If she was naked it would cover her breasts. But that would look silly because her face wasn't classic. It was sharp, nosy, bright. It was white.

"Why do you think your girlfriend left you?" she asked.

"Shouldn't you be writing this down?" said Martin, who would only turn his head. His knees pointed across the hallway at the police bulletin board, which was loaded with red tacks. He saw a flier posted there that said "Ten Pin at the Manitoba Tavern: Battle of the Bands."

"We're just talking, see?" chirped Jane. "I'm going to close your case before it opens, see? Before it becomes a problem for you."

"Who are you?" said Martin. "Are you new? Or something?"

"No."

"Aspiring detective? What is this?"

He managed to be amiable. He had given details to the man behind the counter, after all. Was he supposed to talk to anyone else? This nymph whose belt was on the tightest hole and still looked huge around her waist?

"I'm *trying* to fix it for you," said Jane, reprimanding him pertly. "Do you want your car back? Do you want your girl back?"

"She's been kidnapped," said Martin, tersely. "It was not an escape. She did not run away or leave me. She was forcibly kidnapped and my car was stolen."

"Bullshit. She took your car, drove to Minnesota, and—"

"And what? She didn't have a job, and she didn't take any money."

"So you had animosity toward your girlfriend, because she was unemployed? Did she live with you? Were there money problems? What kind of car was it?" Jane's eyebrows peaked, and her mouth turned down at the corners, a tight smile.

"No, I didn't have any—No there weren't money problems. It was a Buick." Martin frowned, then leaned over and put his hands against the sides of his head, smoothing the slick black hair. His hands were strong, with defined joints, hard skin, veins. His nails were clipped in exact tiny strips above the pink. His hands clenched against his ears.

"I'm sorry," said Jane. "I know it's hard when someone runs out on you, but don't worry. We'll find her, wherever she's gone."

Martin looked up at Jane, suppressing the desire to have sex with her, so that it had to lie idle underneath his desire to rescue Ellen. It would be easier to have sex with Jane than it would be to rescue Ellen, but he loved Ellen, and he did not love Jane. Things that were easy did not fall easily within the realm of duty. Duty included difficulties, absurdities, perplexities, and chores. Which of those categories represented Ellen's necessary rescue, Martin did not know. He certainly hoped that his suicide vision had not forced him into some other realm, where the categories were good and evil, with him a wicked blasphemer, fighting on the side of evil. But that was ridiculous. It wasn't as though he was trying to be some sort of anti-Christ. No. He wanted to have her rescued. He would trudge along and rescue her. He would not waste any time. If this policewoman could facilitate that rescue, as her colleagues would not, then he would work with her, but he would not have sex with her, he decided. That would be wrong.

"She didn't go anywhere. She was taken."

"Alright," she said. "What's your name?"

"Martin."

"Martin, do you want to go somewhere and talk about this case? We could go across the street to the pancake house. Want to?"

Martin stood up and looked down at Jane as she sat still cross-legged on the bench. She did not appear to be seducing him. In fact, she appeared to be brightly, cheerfully, and with absence of guile requesting to offer him her help. She had a fresh look about her, and he now felt that his earlier assumption about her sexual proclivities to be unjust. All female cops did not have to have a mistress thing going on, he decided. This one might be a big-eyed, pointy-chinned, elf-faced virgin, in fact. His sexual interest in her spiked. She was moral.

"Let's go to the pancake house," he said to her, his eyes hooded, his lips forming a straight line. "Do you drink coffee? I'll buy you a coffee."

"I drink coffee," she said.

"Do you want to change clothes first?"

"No," said Jane, "I think it's good for people to see cops wearing their uniforms when they're off duty. I think it instills pride."

"In who?"

"In what."

"In what?"

"Order."

Martin smiled and thought reverently, Order.

In the pancake house, they discussed the relationship of Martin and Ellen. They discussed Ellen's psyche, her peevishness, her delight in surprises, like birthday and Christmas presents.

"She plays a game which is impossible to play," Martin told the rapt Jane. "Months before Christmas she wants to start guessing what her present is, but if you give her an answer that is too indicative, she resents it. For example, if she says, 'Is it made out of minerals,' and I answer, 'Yes,' she rails at me because she knows it's jewelry. The only way to play is for me to invent fantastic and inscrutable clues. And no clue, as you must know in your line of work, is truly inscrutable. Ellen is a professional *scruter*."

Jane laughed, and asked questions about Ellen's dreams, her fantasies, where she wanted to go on their next vacation, if she spoke any foreign languages, the people Ellen knew out of state, where she went to school, if she liked it there, if she ever wanted to go to New York, L.A., Alaska, the Caribbean. She took notes, listing everything down in a little pocket notebook.

"What was her biggest fear?"

"I don't know," said Martin, "I don't imagine she had very many fears. It's possible she feared staying unemployed forever, but we would have gotten married, she would have gotten pregnant, it would have become irrelevant."

"Really."

"She had a fear that she would swallow her engagement ring."

Jane raised her eyebrows, seemed about to giggle, but did not.

"She's not the type of girl to run off with a Buick," said Martin.

"On the contrary. She's just the type."

"You don't even know her," said Martin, almost enjoying talking to this policewoman. He had never allowed himself to go to a shrink.

"You're doing a very good job describing her to me," said Jane. "I'm getting a very clear picture. Listen, here it is. She didn't want to marry you, but she couldn't tell you. She planned to leave, but didn't want to hurt your feelings. She waited until she could make it look like a kidnapping. See? It's all so simple."

Martin made a ring around his coffee cup with his index fingers and thumbs. He felt weird about all this sincerity. He couldn't remember the last time he met someone who felt emotional about employment. In his world, sincerity denoted stupidity. But this girl didn't appear to be stupid.

"Well, if she wanted to leave me...."

"Yes," Jane leaned forward eagerly, expectantly, her relentless eyes wide and alert.

"If she wanted to leave me then I suppose I should just let her go. I don't really mind about the Buick. It's insured, after all. If she really wanted it, the car, and to leave, then she should be allowed to get away. I wouldn't want to run after her. I wouldn't want that," Martin trailed off a bit. He felt alone with this police-woman. Speaking tentatively, sounding unsure: these things were almost refreshing to him. Maybe she knew everything, how everything worked, and he could be muddled for once.

"No!" she exclaimed. "You can't think like that! You have to find her!"

"Why?" said Martin, feeling almost sedated in the vibrancy of her enthusiasm and certainty.

"Well, you can't let her get away with it. You feel abandoned! You feel betrayed! You can't let her do that to you. Have you ever heard of Joan of Arc?"

"WHAT?" cried Martin.

Jane was now sitting on her hands, leaning forward, her police hat casting a shadow over her coffee and the table from the fluorescent lights above. Martin in his black coat laid his hands flat down on the table, and sat back, as if his deal had been made, while she still negotiated. His shoulders pinched together. He had thought of something.

"Why do you want to be on this case?" he asked. "What interest do you have in this particular conflict?"

"Because…," she began. She looked around distractedly, signaled the waitress for the check. Martin reached into his pocket, and laid a five on the table, and signaled the waitress away. Now he turned to raise his eyebrows, and her turn to drag her fingertip around the rim of her coffee cup.

"Because I care!"

Martin nodded kindly, with a gaze equivalent to petting her hair.

"Let's go back to the station," he said, "and see if I can file that report yet."

The police told Martin that his car had been found on the shoulder of I-75, sixteen miles north of Cincinnati, and that it was being examined for evidence.

Chapter Five

Twenty-first century! Commando! Molly! Harrey! Girl warrior! Swoosh!

Molly ran down the basement hallway, her metal boots hitting sharply on the tile. At her sides, arms pumped forward and back. Round hard knees lifted her legs up and down, pushing the heavy pleats of her thick gray skirt. She wore blue reflective glasses for secrecy, high short ponytails for illusion, a tight gray t-shirt for shock. She wore a charm bracelet. Her imaginary gun was holstered, leaving her tanned little fists clenched and empty.

Think! Remember! Observe! Ocular implants click! Mechanical joints click! Swivel neck!

Molly allowed her last stride to become a leap, and landed with her feet planted. She placed her right boot behind her and executed a ninety-degree military turn to the right. Glancing up and down the hallway, she stepped carefully backward until her back touched the wall right beside the door. She drew her imaginary gun from its holster slowly, making a gun shape with her right hand, index finger pointing, clasping her right wrist with her left fist to steady the weapon.

Clamp! Stance! Feet spread two feet apart! Left foot points to ten o'clock! Right foot points to two o'clock! Just! Like! Violin class!

Molly placed her left foot precisely into the doorway, jutting her toes up against the closed door, twisting her leg around. Her back to the wall, she could see this way, that way, then in a motion of pulling her right leg around, she turned one hundred and eighty degrees, landing face straight to the door, her hands clasped in front of her breasts. She made the fake gun point with both her index fingertips, and it pointed at her chin.

Breathe in! Out! Homeostasis! Systems! Functional! Hallway secure! Approaching! Tunnel!

Life was like a banal tragic misbegotten screenplay with no action, no love story, no explosions, no high-speed chases, no global warfare, no hero, no villain, no victim. It was all plaintive talk and scenes without movement. Of this screenplay, critics would say, "Where is the plot?" or possibly, "This movie dragged" and "I fell asleep and died because of the severe boredom I was experiencing" and maybe they would even say "What this movie needs is an exceptionally cute cyborg heroine who runs down hallways and leaps into door frames, carrying a deadly gun." For Molly, life stretched back to the point where she had been sitting very still in the choir loft amid many other little choir children, watching the struggling boy acolyte who was trying to light the altar candles with his long instrument, hearing the Lutheran Pastor hiss "Lengthen your wick" from his hidden seat behind the lectern. For Molly, life stretched forward into a misty future, where she was part human, part machine, all deadly calm and violence, a stiff mercenary who could be bought, tricked, wooed, won. Yes, she was a phantasm from the future, and she dressed for the part.

Tunnels! Oil drums! Dirty! Concrete! The prisoner! Huddles! In the cell!

Molly reached down with her left hand and lifted the latch on the door, turned the door handle. Keeping the door handle turned until the moment of impact, which was awkward but necessary, she kicked the door wide open with her foot, and stood in the blaze of light from the tunnel. The girl inside stood staring blankly at her, hands half raised. It looked like she had recently combed her hair with her fingers, and the hair now hung in flat chunks around her face. She was tall and pretty and looked like a scaredypants. Molly sighed in satisfaction. Her fake gun was in her right hand, and her left hand propped up her elbow as she pointed it straight at the girl.

"You pissed yourself!" Molly hollered. "I can smell it!"

The girl was staring at Molly's pointing hand, wrinkling up her forehead.

"I've been down here for three days," she said, "I couldn't help it."

"You've been down here for five minutes!" Molly barked. "Three days? What an assumption! What a grand delusion! You!"

The girl's face, though not paralyzed by fear, had at least lost that quizzical, almost amused expression.

Bionic thrusters! Armed! Cataclysm device! Ready! Communication with mortals! Difficult!

"Get down on the floor," Molly said sharply. The girl stretched out on the floor, on her stomach, cautiously and without much briskness. Molly breathed in deeply and then placed a foot on the back of the girl's neck.

"What's your name?"

"Ellen," said the girl, sounding strangled.

"And who do you work for, Ellen?"

I'll never! Reveal! That! You'll have to! Torture me! Don't worry! That! Can be! Arranged!

"What?" said the girl, shifting around under Molly's boot.

"Never mind," said Molly. "You work for us now, is that clear? You work for us now!"

"Who are you?" asked Ellen.

"Shut up!" Molly yelled, picking up the rope from the floor. She wrapped it in a loop and stowed it in her pocket, replacing the restraints on Ellen's wrists with a stiff pair of handcuffs which had been hanging from her belt. She snapped the handcuffs tight, "And get up!"

Ellen struggled to her feet.

"Come with me!" Molly put her left hand around the handcuffs and pushed Ellen in front of her, toward the door. Her right hand, index finger pointing into Ellen's back, thumb pointed to the ceiling, shook just a bit.

Ellen walked stiffly in front of Molly, and Molly's eyes were on the level of Ellen's shoulder blades. They walked in this way out of the tunnel and down the hallway, which was a basement hallway of a large building. They passed big network servers covered in plastic, heaps of office furniture, doors on the left and right side. They came to the marble foyer and the elevator. Ellen seemed cowed and silent. Molly straightened up, still holding her hand as a gun into Ellen. Inside the elevator, Molly punched the button marked with a star for the first floor.

"Believe me," said Molly, "if you move or call to anyone, or make any noise at all, I will have you out the front door within thirty seconds, and it's not going to be pretty when we get in the car."

Ellen looked at her and half-smiled. Molly didn't smile back. It was to be serious in the elevator. There would be no smiling. There would be no yelling. There would be no struggle. There would be an efficacious gun, and a gentle prisoner, and time would flow quickly along, and events would come at an even pace, and the progression would be smooth, from prisoner, to hostage, to wife. It would be a smooth progression, and interesting.

Many! Have been killed! In the freight! Elevator! Security cameras! Traps! Lights! Designs on the Imperial Throne! Murder!

When the elevator doors opened smoothly onto a bright lobby, two stories high, with trees and pots of bushes, red carpeting thrown over shining marble, polished brass lighting fixtures, simple sculptures and huge windows, the girl beside Molly breathed in deeply and seemed to sag a bit. Molly scanned the lobby. It was quiet. Seven o'clock in the evening and the receptionist was still there, chewing on a pen, looking at a quiet black phone. The airiness of the lobby was dangerous, Molly knew. But she was sure they would not be disturbed. Would not be interrupted.

In the fortress! Of the Most High! In the Emperor's Castle! Hot oil! Mr. Clean! Nod! To the border guard! Show! The pass! Revise! Speech to the prisoner! It is all! Understood! In this metal haven! Where radio waves do not! Mean! A thing! Violence! Gloom! Surrender! Never! All! In the protective! Carapace! Of the Empire! Click! The prisoner wilts! She shudders! The barrel is slick! Polished! And there is motor oil! Everywhere! It has been spilled! By tanks! There the immense clanking doors! There the reinforced steel is not a window! There the monster in his cavern is below! For the Cyborg warrior! This! Is! Home base! Salute the border guard! Who understands! The importance! Of this mission! We! Drink! Wine! Out of skins! And we shit glass!

"Hello, Miss Harrey," said the receptionist languidly, putting down her pen.

"Hello, June," said Molly, smiling at her. They stopped for a moment in front of the giant reception desk, made of dark wood, edged in the polished brass that was ubiquitous in the room.

"Is that your friend?" asked June.

"Yes," said Molly, "This is my friend. Would you like to meet her?"

Molly was feeling delicious. She shoved her arm in Ellen's elbow forward, presenting her to June.

"Sarah, meet June," said Molly.

"Hi, Sarah," said June with all the sugar she could muster, poor June.

"Hi," said Ellen. Ellen looked like she could use a cheeseburger.

"Well, June," said Molly kindly, "We need to be moving along now. Sarah is going to meet Jay tonight. We don't want to be late."

"Alright then," said June. "It was nice meeting you, Sarah."

"Nice to meet you too," said Ellen.

Recognition! By retinal scan! The border guard! A renegade professional! The prisoner! Hopeless! There! Is! No! Mercy! Here! It will all come out! The treason! The betrayal! She will be absorbed! Functional! Useful! Through! The clanking doors! Into! The paddock! That! Is what we call it! It keeps everything! Ready! Into! The transport! To! The Castle! Of the prince! The prince! Interrogation! No! I will never tell you! You cannot! Break me! Kill me! I will not! Repent! You! Will! Confess! Or you! Will go back! To your cell! Immediately! There! Are! Shooters! In every window! Aiming! Killers!

Molly steered Ellen toward her car, toward the door of the car, and Ellen walked alongside peacefully, first one foot and then the other down the parking lot, just like she should, Molly knew. Molly went click on the car door, staring into Ellen's face.

"You will not try anything tricky in the car," Molly said. "You will just sit there and mind your own business, because when I'm driving, I don't want to be holding a gun on you, and I can't have you pulling on me, because I have to drive. So don't do anything in the car but just sit there. I am serious about this. Jay will be very mad at you if you're not good in the car; he won't like you. I promise you this. I ask you twenty times to be good in the car, because if you hurt me in any way, Jay will kill you. That will happen. Don't be confused about that point."

Molly! Is! Driving! Click click! Porsche! In the transport! Is everything! Exceptional! Technology! It roars! It chimes! It is state of the art! Ten corners! Eighteen stop lights! Seventeen pedestrians! It! All! Computes! It's a ninety-five miles-per-hour party on four wheels! The prisoner! A white! Shadow! Because this! Is! Her! Machine! Now she takes on! A form incarnate! With edges! That are sharp! And deadly! The prisoner! Is shocked! At the speed!

Ellen looked scared beside Molly who was driving. "Who is Jay?" she said. "Who is this Jay? Where are you taking me?"

Molly didn't want anything terrible or irritating to happen until they got to Jay's house. She wanted her part of the mission to be smoothly completed, without error, without regression, without terror.

"It's not important," she said to Ellen. "Look, Jay's going to be your husband. So you will find out eventually. Don't let the suspense eat at you or anything."

"My husband?" said Ellen. "What is this?"

"Look, what would you do right now if I just OPENED THE DOOR AND GOT OUT AT THE NEXT STOPLIGHT?" Molly bellowed, "I COULD JUST GET OUT OF THE CAR YOU KNOW."

"That's not a real gun," said Ellen. "You don't have anything."

"Well gosh," said Molly, red in the cheeks but speaking smoothly, "We're only going to Jay's house. I haven't taken you anywhere yet."

The gears! Whir! In her head! It makes a hurt! If there can be! One!

Molly's cell phone rang inside the glove compartment. She leaned over Ellen to get it out and answered it, flipping open the clasp and taking her eyes off the road to glare at Ellen for a long moment.

.

.

.

...Incoming Transmission from the Prince of Knives...

.

.

.

Begin Transmission

.

.

.

Have you secured the prisoner? Good, I am waiting. I am pleased with you, Girl Warrior. You have done well. I am experiencing uncertainty as to our procedure from this point in the mission. I have decided to receive the prisoner in the Castle, rather than the Outpost as was originally agreed. And at your discretion, you may require the prisoner to be blinded for her approach. Please inform the prisoner that she is welcome in my realm, and that no harm will come to her as long as she is not resistant to our schedules. Please ask the prisoner to remain calm. Please reassure her. Please do not harm the prisoner in any way. Please do not subject the prisoner to any unnecessary risk by operating your transport at unsafe speeds. Please apologize to the prisoner on my behalf for any discomfort she may have experienced while in the holding cell. Please do not cause the prisoner any emotional discomfort by withholding from her the details of your mission. Please do not neglect to provide the prisoner with any physical comfort she may require, such as a soda or cheeseburger. Please make all haste to the Castle where we will formulate our course of action from this point.

.

.

.

...End Transmission...

.

.

.

Click! The Prince of Knives! Is! Happy! He is wait-
ing! The physical comfort! Of the prisoner! Is! Paramount!
She must arrive safe at the castle! She! Is! To! Be! Princess!
And someday Queen!

"Where's your coat?" Molly asked Ellen as they
careened around a sharp corner and came up the hill
into Perrysburg.

"Oh," said Ellen, "I must have left it in the tunnel. I thought we were, going South. It seemed warm.
I didn't think I'd need it."

"No," said Molly. "You had it in the elevator. What
did you do with it?"

"I left it in the tunnel," said Ellen. "I remember
taking it off and leaving it there."

Molly sighed, rolled her eyes, and made it clear
that she did not believe Ellen. People who are lying
should not be allowed to believe they are good at lying. They should be made to think that they are not
successful. That way, they will be more likely to come
through with the truth eventually. Lying is a bad trait.

"Well, he said he's sorry you had to piss yourself."

"You didn't have to tell him that," Ellen said.

"What do you care?"

"Anyway, I didn't piss myself like piss myself, I
just had to go to the bathroom," Ellen said.

"Whatever," said Molly. "He also wants you
blinded, and we're going somewhere different, so I'll
blind you before we get on the freeway."

Ellen pulled at the handcuffs, as if trying to touch
her shoulders together in the front, and sort of leaned

over in her seat, appearing cold. She was a weak specimen, unlikely, dry.

The! Future! Princess! Sits! Boldly! In! Hostility! She! Cannot! Be! Broken!

"Are you hungry?" asked Molly.

"Yes," said Ellen, whose forehead was almost resting on her knee.

"Would you like to go to Roy Rogers? There's one just before we get on the freeway."

"Where are we going on the freeway?" asked Ellen again, almost folded in half and looking so stupid, her hair falling down on her legs sloppily.

"Sit UP!" barked Molly. "If food will help you act a little more cheerful, then I'm going to feed you! If anyone could benefit from a metallic exoskeleton, it's you!"

Try! This! The remote! Trading Post! Corner of! The universe! Left! At Mars! Ha ha! Feed her meat! Protein! A bleak! Sustenance! To be sure! But nectar! Soon enough!

"I'm just trying to be nice to you," Molly explained, in a kind and gracious tone of which Jay would surely approve. She must practice loving Ellen, after all. She must become so accustomed to it that it would be almost a pleasure to love her. If only she had more spirit. If only she had more spunk. It was sucking all the life out of Molly just to maintain a festive attitude in the presence of this dry, pensive, mucky girl. Maybe Jay would be tired of her within minutes of their arrival. Maybe he would send her right back.

"Where are we going?" Ellen asked again doggedly.

"Look around you!" Molly said loudly, her eyes wide and insistent, because she was hating how dense this girl was. "Do you see where you are? You're in Perrysburg, Ohio. Have you ever been here before? I believe you live about forty-five minutes from here. The similarity between this Perrysburg and the one you are accustomed to is so STRIKING, so OVERWHELMING, that they are almost one and the same city! In fact, they exactly are!"

"Perrysburg," said the girl, sitting up and looking out the window. She sighed deeply and frowned. "I thought we would be in Kentucky at least. Why did you bring me back here?"

"Bring you back? He never left, princess. You've been right here in Northwest Ohio all along. He just drove you down south, dumped your car, got in his car, and came right back up. Isn't that obvious?"

Ellen leaned back against the seat, her elbows going cockeyed as the handcuffs pulled her wrists together. She shoved her knees against the dashboard, ignoring the view from the window.

"Don't you think that Martin will find me here?" she said quietly, meanly. "I mean, he's less than an hour away from us right now."

Silence! In the Pleasure Dome! Traitors! In the Green Room! Psionic Blasters! Click! Shields! Up! Defensive Matrix resolved! Plot! Course! Of the Resistance! Sir, they are moving in a circle! Blind! As! I! Thought! Mutations! Will! Not! Prevail! Against our Evolution!

Molly chuckled.

"Martin isn't going to find you here. No one will ever find you. No, they will not find you, because you will not be found. You're going to be happy, Ellen. You'll be happy deep in the halls of…you'll be happy and safe with Jay. They won't get in."

"Who is Jay?"

They had pulled into the parking lot of the Roy Rogers. Molly turned to Ellen and explained that just for the purpose of getting some food, they would not need the gun, because Ellen would be good and quiet, and obviously, she wanted to know what was going on, and she never would know if she made any suspicious noises, so could Ellen be trusted? Could Molly leave the gun in the car? Would they be able to eat a civilized cheeseburger together without incident?

Ellen agreed that they could. Molly sighed and nodded, seeing how her hands fit right around the steering wheel, as if the steering wheel had been made for hands just like hers. Ellen got out of the car and waited for her to get out, almost as if they were already sisters. Molly carefully placed the fake gun in the back seat and covered it with a blanket. She saw Ellen watching her and remembered to be discreet in this way. As they walked in, Molly reminded Ellen that she was wearing handcuffs. Probably the girl was getting so comfortable in her new life that she had already forgotten them. However, there they were, and they couldn't come off. Molly told Ellen to just say how they had been playing around, and had lost the key, if anyone asked. They stopped outside the Roy Rogers to practice this possibly necessary exchange.

"Why do you have handcuffs on?" asked Molly, impersonating someone in the restaurant.

"Oh, we were just playing around and we lost the key," Ellen replied, shrugging her shoulders a bit. Then she added, "Isn't it funny?"

"Yes, isn't it funny? We were just playing around," said Molly, in a Molly tone of voice. Then she dropped her voice to serious again, "Okay, you did fine. Just remember to smile."

Molly reached for the door, opened it, and they went in. Sitting at a table in the Roy Rogers, Molly fed Ellen her food. This was necessary because Ellen's hands were tied behind her with handcuffs.

Nothing! Comes! Without a price! Including! Your food! For this! A confession! For that! A new promise! This is a trade! My sensors! Report! Your! Systems! Weakening! What's this! Hunger! Ha! For me! Data! In the Trading Post! Are many enemies! Of the Realm! All! Enemies! Are allies! Today! Transients! Bend! Unite! Form a line!

Ellen ate slowly, chewing each thing Molly put into her mouth. It was tiresome to feed the girl while she herself wasn't eating. It was a sacrifice of her time and energy. Ellen seemed to really enjoy the food, but she also said it was going to make her sick. Molly knew that many girls were like this, eating too much and then talking immediately about nausea. Molly wondered what Ellen would look like when she was cleaned up and in a party dress, or what she would look like naked. If Jay wondered this, when he saw her, then it would be a success. He couldn't help but wonder. He would have to imagine this girl as sexy. Strangely enough no one asked them about the handcuffs.

"You still haven't told me who Jay is," Ellen reminded her, after she had sucked from the straw in the cup that Molly lifted to her mouth.

.

.

.

...accessing file...jay.smr...file retrieved... loading...

.

.

.

Every child born into Western Civilization must repeat its history as he becomes a man. Jay is a man, and therefore, he has repeated the history of Western Civilization. At the age of six months, Jay recognized himself as an individual, and lost his innate connection with the collective universe, with Gaia, with the folkloric consciousness, with the Oversoul, and all that horseshit with which innocents and civilizations are born. Moving thus and so straightforward from the folk into the self, as did the ancients move from public into private life, constructing boundaries, experiencing life as a single being, he developed subsequent unique connections with particular other human beings, these being our mother and our father. He invented and mastered a system of signs and symbols common to that social group, which was refined with outside contact to conform to a language common to the larger group of his community. He learned to write. And read. Learned a counting structure, and simple math. He experienced at first local and then increasingly wide circles of travel. Around the age of six he shifted from the Ptolemic conception of the solar system to the Galilean. That is, he came to understand that the universe didn't revolve around him, goddammit, that there was a great big Milky Way out there, with lots of stars, and that his planet body was just one of several, revolving around one of many, revolving around ten-thousand billion of same and different, and he was very small. I like to pretend that the birth of myself had some small influence on this paradigm shift, but I digress. The forgotten and dark ages of eight, nine, and ten were followed by the enlightenment and romanticism of the pre-teen years. At this time Jay moved from the feudal system of the patriarchal family into the larger and more exciting world of the high-school work force, and he learned to operate heavy machinery for a small wage. The industrial revolution—do you see? Soon after this, he made his first solo flight. Following this there were several wars. Internal hierarchies were established. Existentialism peaked and waned. He realized he could kill himself. He refrained from doing it.

As his technological knowledge and ability advanced through study and practice and a university education in electrical engineering and computer programming, he jutted clearly and vibrantly into the present day, with all of its wires, and its presence of mind, and global connectivity. Jay is a modern, he is a contemporary, he is a post-contemporary, and in his extreme state of advancement he has suffered as we all do now the disjunction of mind and body, the isolation, the dependence on machine, the insufferable indignity of the unloved Cyborg, crucified on his own coaxial cable, because it has all gotten so out of control.

It is a great responsibility that he bravely shoulders for all of us, as he forges what is the next step for all of us, the reconnectivity, the assimilation of the Cyborg self. In learning to love his prosthesis, in delivering the damned into the social community of the informed, in creating our new heaven, for all of us, he inscribes it with all these ultramodern appliances and credos amid love and desire and all kinds of reforged human emotions. Why should a man stop his evolution at 26, because the world has stopped? This is his mission, as we have deciphered it.

.

.

.

...save file...close file...

.

.

.

The two girls sat in the Roy Rogers, one hand-feeding the other, and Molly delivered her information, all that was necessary, all that was helpful, to Ellen out of her brain, so that the transition would be swift and easy and good. Of course, she would maintain constant surveillance until the mission was complete or the girl was dead. It was her duty to Jay.

Speak! Quietly! Hushed tones! For there are plants! And listeners! Even here! With this! The primary objective! Is met! To deliver the prisoner! To the Prince of Knives! And to prove her initiation! And her introduction! For the Evolution! We all fight!

Chapter Six

Jay lay with his arms spread on the kitchen floor in the house that he had purchased for himself and the girl, a glowing house of light and light tan tile, light and light yellow walls, and wood floors, a fireplace, a generous staircase, glass, a bright cement driveway, a copper roof over one gable, a yard, a subdivision, a suburb, a city, a world. The house he had chosen had been recently built. He picked a dark green one, in a familiar city, in a new neighborhood, with white trim, and white eaves, if that's what those things were called, white doors and windows, white down onto the floor he was lying on, down to the tile on which his face was pressed, which was on its side, the face, and mashed down against the tile, where he could feel it was cold, and feel the texture of its whiteness, and he thought he would hang a stained glass thingy on the patio door, with maybe a hummingbird on it or maybe a unicorn, which would be stupid but perfect, and he would learn to love it.

From here in this house in this world, he remembered the surroundings from which he had recently arisen, a black basement, network of wires and cables, SCSI, serial, all this big system from port to port was stretched and taped across ceilings, a microfridge full of soda cans and upstairs Mother and Father lived in their house which was called an estate, on the yard which was called a grounds, behind the driveway which was called a drive. Behind trees, behind wilderness, beside a lake plenty far from the rest of humanity, all capsuled up underneath there in his basement, which his mother wanted to redecorate and which his father wanted to light up with a match and explode.

Jay closed his eyes in the kitchen of his new house, and he imagined the girl gliding back and forth between refrigerator and stove and dining room table, and himself gulping coffee at the counter in preparation for a day at the office, and children thundering down the stairs. There would be potholders and small machines like coffee makers and can openers, a dishwasher humming, mother looking forward to the peace of cleaning up this mess, and smiling, and forgiving, and wearing an apron—or if that was too much then a housecoat and robe, or a housecoat or a robe. It would be purple plush, and tied at the waist, and underneath would be visible a white nightgown, and mother would look very different in the mornings than she did at company picnics, or at dinner parties. She would look so vulnerable, and the father, kissing her on his way out, would spend an extra second holding her because of this, squeezing her up to him with the kids impatiently waiting at the door, anxious to get to school, squabbling in the distance.

Jay stretched his arms out as far as they would go on the linoleum floor and sighed deeply, looking straight up into the ceiling and shutting his eyes. "I love you this much," he said. "I love you THIS much." In the kitchen the mother was saying, "Of course the most important element of chicken fried rice is the egg! Otherwise, it's just rice and chicken!"

Life is like an empty box. You can fill it with a Novell Network, and a basement and an orange rug, and seventeen hours a day online, and a new protocol that really beats TCP/IP and even NetBios, and an LPMUD, and a stack of Mountain Dew cans carefully arranged to look like a map of the former USSR, and that would be hateful, bad, and disappointing, and you would want to kill yourself, hate yourself, purge yourself, because it has all turned out badly. There are too many things in your box that make you horrible, unpleasant, that make you drive a ruined Volvo, that make you stop before you speak, shuffle, delete, return. There are things in the box that you want to pick up and throw into the garbage, wipe it, clean it, spray it with strong disinfectant detergent, hold it under the waterfall until it is clean and clear, and then, you can look into your empty box, and the way you have always thought the box would be filled is now again clearly possible.

You can put in a house in the suburbs. You can put in a pretty wife. You can put in your college degree again, but this time you can put it next to an office on the 45th floor, one that says Junior Vice President outside the door, and then when you go up to your father's big office in the penthouse, and slide by his receptionist, you won't be wearing dirty jeans, and you won't be coming to tell him to stop using the server to check his dailies. You will be coming to say that you closed the Dawson account and that the clients are ecstatic, that the lunch meeting was a success, and you will be wearing a dark tie, and you will be indistinguishable from the ninety other junior VPs spread out like dots across the country and in London and

Helsinki, there will be other counterparts to you, but you will be his son, because that is what you have always been, except now instead of hiding in the basement, instead of horsing around with the code junkies down in the pit, or taking a trip to the Houston office to write some new proprietary software for UNIX, or set up a mail server, you will be going to meet with people, real people. Now when you look into your box it is a proud box, a healthy box, a box which has just recently been sent to the dry cleaner and is now divided evenly by each careful crease.

Jay looked at his watch to see what time it was. If Molly had picked up the girl at seven o'clock, she should have arrived over half an hour ago. Maybe there had been a problem. Maybe the girl was not safe. Maybe Molly had smashed up the car and was now dead. The watch was a Star Trek: The Next Generation watch, which had at one time been ironic but was now ridiculous. He removed the watch from his wrist and stood up slowly, holding it in one hand. Walking over to the kitchen counter, he picked up the wrought iron free-standing paper towel dispenser that he had bought himself as a house-warming present, and smashed the watch into fragments on the counter. Of course the band was still intact. He swept the pieces of watch into his hand and considered the garbage, considered the garbage disposal, considered the back door, but really, nothing was possible, because what if the girl arrived, and needed to throw away a tissue, or needed to garbage-dispose a carrot top, or walked outside and saw the remnants of this Star Trek watch, and saw the very obvious typeface, then what? He had put a lot of effort into the khaki pants and the light denim shirt. He had worn black soft boots and had brushed his hair down so that it looked casual. But if she saw this watch remnant, she might instantly intuit that when he was crouched over a dissected motherboard, he used to wear this very same hair in a high ponytail on top of his head, and eat Pop-Tarts unheated, and forget to change his socks. There was nothing in the house. Nothing had been moved in except in the girl's room upstairs. If there was a potted plant, he could dig in the dirt and bury the watch under the roots. If there was a box of CD's he could put the bits into it, and say, "Oh, this old thing. It got crushed. How I do love to remember High School."

At this moment, the doorbell rang its gentle and familiar three-toned ring, something he had dreamed about, and now could not enjoy. At the last minute he shoved the pieces of watch into his pocket, and he heard the female voices coming into the hallway. Molly had just opened the door and come right in, not waiting for him to come to the door. This is how it would now be forever, because Molly would naturally always have a key; only when she walked right in, in the future, it would have to be to this scene: Jay and Ellen in front of the television, happily sipping at iced tea, finished with the day, tired of the phone, catching up on the evening news, gently sparring about a baseball score, Jay would be in his robe, and Ellen's hair would be wet from the shower, and they would be sitting, right there, right exactly there as he could see into the front room from the kitchen, and mark it out on the empty floor. "Who's here," Ellen would say merrily, and Jay would reply that it was only Molly. Ellen would ask if Molly wanted anything to drink. Molly would sit on the floor with her boots under her butt. Molly would say, "Daddy is so pleased with your work at the company," and Jay would say something and write out a check and say, "This should cover rent for a few months—now stop feeling dependent on that boyfriend of yours." Except that Molly wasn't dependent on a boyfriend, and she had lots of money, and there weren't any chairs for them to sit in, and there was no television, and Jay didn't even like baseball. Molly and Ellen came through the kitchen doorway.

"Ellen, this is Jay," said Molly tartly. Molly marched over to him and pressed her hand against his, and he figured out that she was passing her pretend gun over to him, expecting him to make a fake gun with his hand now, and he put his index finger out halfheartedly, not really paying attention, because he was looking at Ellen. Molly said that she had to go to the bathroom and went upstairs.

"Hello Ellen," he said.

"You're not the one from the car. Are you Jay?" she asked.

Now that Ellen stood in front of him he felt very uncertain and very nonplussed. This girl standing in front of him was quite perfectly beautiful and real. She was tall, with light brown hair, and she was willowy and she had grace. She had long legs and ankles. She had a chin and a neck and she was looking at him. He wondered if he could depend on this girl to love him, if he could pull her close to him right now and if she would come, if she would slide right into him. And if she would start right away with loving him, and if he would be hers and she his, and if this wife that he now had would be happy, and if she would have a happy life, which were things he had not discussed with himself previously to this meeting, when she was suddenly fleshy, more than an apron, more than a pair of reading glasses left on a feminine nightstand in his mind, when she was this gorgeous girl with amazingly clear eyes and she belonged to him on the basis of the fact that he had her now in his house and she could never be allowed to leave if that's what he decided, and instead of moving like an automaton, propping for his role as husband, he now wanted her to be a true believer, to participate in a romance, to love him.

His mother had explained to him the way that women love. "A woman can love any man who loves her first," she had said. "That is how it was with me and your father. Because he was in love with me, and because he had what I knew myself to want, I loved him, and it was true, and real." Jay wanted to feel himself believe this fact, and set himself from now to forever to love this Ellen truly, and to have what she wanted to have, and thus to make her love him with the same peaceful sincerity that his mother loved the old man. She stood in the doorway between the foyer and the kitchen, slightly slouched. She was resting one ankle by putting her weight onto the other foot. Of course he would love this girl.

Of course, there was the fact that everything he felt was virtual horseshit, and he was nervous and depressed and feeling everything he'd always felt while in a room with a pretty girl, even the resentment and hostility, certainly not any attribute that connected him to this house he was in. If he were to open his mouth and say something, it would be stupid, and she would answer stupidly, proving this was an enormous mistake, and proving that she would have to go back. But he willed himself to be here, in this clean life, all purged, and the new way was to be sure, and talkative, and right, and to feel himself as full of power, and certain, and good.

So he said, "I'm Jay. Molly's my sister. No, I'm not the one who took you from the 7-Eleven. That was Molly's boyfriend. He was doing it for us. It's actually terribly funny. See, he overheard us saying something, and he interpreted it as a plan. See, we said that if I ever expected to get a wife, then someone would have to kidnap a wife for me. I guess...I guess I'm just that way. So he did this thing, which I suppose we sort of wanted him to do on some level, though not overtly, and there it had been done, and we had to decide exactly what to do about it, and so here you are, and it's very nice meeting you, and probably now you can leave."

Molly came thundering down the stairs.

"What? No, she can't. What's the matter with you."

Ellen looked confused and hurt, as if she didn't want to leave. "He hit me," said Ellen, "in the head."

"Oh, no no," said Jay. "He can't have hit you. He's Molly's boyfriend. He wouldn't hit you. Molly, would he hit her?"

The house made noises like a new empty house covered in a thin film of dust. It felt uncertain, creaky, empty. Jay felt immediately that they had to let the girl go.

"He may have clobbered her a little bit," said Molly briskly, grabbing Ellen's handcuffs and pulling her out into the foyer and toward the stairs.

"What?" cried Jay, running after them. "He HIT her? She can leave now, Molly, because *we* did not kidnap her. And we did not *want* her kidnapped. We didn't want her *kidnapped*."

"Look, he was kidnapping her," Molly shot back, pulling Ellen up the stairs. "If it got nasty at her end, it's not his fault. She should have just let him. Now I'm going to put her upstairs. We'll talk about it later."

"Molly, she can go now."

"Why can't she stay?"

"We don't kidnap people, Molly. It was a joke. Maybe a nice idea. But we don't kidnap people."

"Why don't we?" said Molly. "Why aren't we running around kidnapping girls every living second, using them for our pleasure, and then leaving them for dead in Mexico City?"

"Stop it," Jay said sharply, frowning. "With every word you say this is more irreversible. She doesn't know who took her. She doesn't know us. We take her into town, take her back. Nothing happens. We can do things the normal way. We can."

"She's going to have a wonderful life, Jay. So are you," Molly pulled Ellen along, and Ellen was looking like she wanted to go upstairs, stay, live forever. She also looked scared, miserable, desperate, and confused.

"Molly, don't be overbearing, and don't decide, make decisions and predictions in such a forthright and rigid tone," Jay broke in. "It was a mistake—"

"A mistake," said Ellen. "What?"

"Forget it," said Molly to Ellen. "He's not himself."

"It was a mistake. You go home, you forget, we forget."

Ellen paused, about to say something, and chewed her lip. She pulled away from Molly and steadied herself on the stairs. "No," she said, hesitantly at first and then building resolution. "If you plan on letting me go, then realize immediately that I will prosecute you to the full extent of the law, and my boyfriend Martin will not rest until he finds you, and you will go to jail." She stood up straighter, and there was a bit of hysteria in her voice now as she said, "I will most certainly run straight to the police and make things very ugly for you! I think I have to vomit! I think I am going to scream!"

Molly slapped her hand over Ellen's mouth and shoved her head back against the wall, and nodded at Jay.

"You see?" she said. "We have absolutely no choice but to see this thing through. You're marrying her, and she's going to love it."

Jay stared at Ellen, where her eyes were kind of bugging out over Molly's pressed fingers, and he thought he saw her looking at him as if he was her savior, as if he could explain everything, as if she was only hoping to be alone with him, so that he could show her how things would be, so that he could lay it out for her. No one would hit her anymore. She would be a rich woman. She would be happy here in their house with him together.

He said slowly, "I really do want to take her back. This is so completely—I really do not want to proceed. It can all be actualized in some other way, some less dramatic way, without the handcuffs and all your screaming."

"You don't want to take her back, you fucking pussy," said Molly. "You want to take her upstairs and pet her hair and give her a bath and slap a ring on her. Don't be a fucking pussy for one fucking moment of your life. And don't play dumb, pussy. What did you fix that tunnel for? A bomb shelter?"

A key turned in the lock. The door opened and Stef walked in.

"Hi," he said.

Molly said, "Hi honey," and then turned to glare at Jay triumphantly.

Stef saw Ellen and said, "Oh shit. I thought she was in the tunnel until tomorrow. I'll, uh…wait in the car. Shit."

He turned quietly, stepped back onto the porch, and closed the door behind him. Jay saw the night outside disappear and looked at Molly.

"So now what?" said Molly, flipping her hair back. "You still want to take her back?"

Jay shook his head, how could Stef have come in here, how could it all be set into motion in this way, but it was, undeniably, set into motion, and she was here, after all, available, and maybe there was no choice, and maybe she really wanted to be here, if that could be believed, then anything was possible, including this.

Molly turned without waiting for an answer and dragged the girl up the stairs. He sat down on the bottom step and waited for Molly to come back down. She would have to arrange Ellen's room, make sure everything was perfect, organize the toilet and the bath, fix her up with shampoo, washcloths, everything. Molly had brought it all in, pretending that they would actually do it. And Stef had pretended that it was a mistake. They had confused him. It wasn't his fault. It was his chance.

Molly returned down the stairs and sat down beside him, putting her arm around him and letting her head fall down on his shoulder.

"Jay, it's all going to be fine," she said, rubbing her hand against his knee. "I just love her. She's perfect."

"Do you think so?" he said.

"Well don't you?" Molly said, pushing her head into his neck and rubbing harder, insistently on his knee. Maybe she had never seen him in khaki pants before. Maybe she had, when he was in prep school. Of course she had.

"She now thinks I am crazy, or retarded, or that I have strange ideas at least, and in the least she is right in that I failed to anticipate this development, because I am looking at it this way, and she that way, with only the picture up to one point, whereas I have the picture beyond that point, although not as far as you apparently had carried it, you and Stef together, and so while the symmetry was clear to me, it escaped her entirely, and left her with this, you know, impression of me as a lunatic, which caused her to address me sharply, and talk about Police, as if I were being silly, or she had to straighten me out, or something, which did not impress me, I mean if she is caustic or hostile, that's not good, but if I provoked it, then it's on my shoulders. I'm just more interested in sending her back. It's obvious I was right in that respect. I mean I don't think it can really work out, if such a ridiculous thing as a house in the suburbs can set it off in such harsh tones, such a gross misunderstanding, do you see? So we will take her back instead. She was really hostile, Moll. I think she hates us."

While he spoke, Molly nodded gravely, turning at intervals to look at the floor, and then turning back to Jay with great attention. She was really adorable, Jay thought, like a little doll with her ponytails. It was impossible to believe that she had orchestrated this,

that she was a maniac, capable of kidnapping someone. She was always out ahead of him, always, but to
this point she hadn't changed his life. Now she had.
Next to Jay and his height and long limbs, she looked
as if she could be picked up and played with.

Jay sighed. He said, "It's never a good idea to kidnap someone. He was really, in retrospect quite wrong
to do it. And we should have made that clear, in telling him, and I should have just let her out, given her
dinner, said goodbye. We may as well let her go. Even
now, as she is upstairs getting ready for bed, she is
deciding in her mind that—that she's not going to like
this experience. She was standing here looking at me
and my scary gun here, and thinking how she could
have done this or that to avoid us, or if she hadn't gone
out yesterday, or if she had lived in a different country,
or anything, just so she wasn't standing there, on my
new stairs."

"Nonsense, no," Molly interrupted briskly,
"You're wrong and everything's going to be fine. I'm
sure she already likes you a lot."

"Well," said Jay, feeling tired, "I was thinking
when you walked in here that she was absolutely perfect, but now, what if she's angry with us? What if she
doesn't really want to stay?"

Molly stood up and walked toward the door.

"I have to go talk to Stef. I'm sure he feels bad
about coming in here. Listen to me—don't go in that
room. I will be back tomorrow before my class. I do
not want you going in there. She's peed, she's had food,
she doesn't need anything. Don't go mooning over her
while she's sleeping and then leave the door unlocked.
I'll be really pissed."

"Okay," said Jay.

Molly smiled at him from the door, and then she
left him alone with the girl.

Chapter Seven

Martin sat in his office at The Joyride with his hand on the phone. He absolutely had to call Ellen's family immediately and tell them what had happened. The unfortunate thing, the troublesome thing, beyond the guilty fact of Ellen's having disappeared, was that Ellen's father was slightly retarded. Speaking to him on the phone or in person filled Martin with the deepest dread, the most terrible angst, and great physical discomfort. It wasn't that Ellen's father drooled, or talked about little gnomes that came into his room at night with drums and horns. The retardation was not severe. He fed himself, urinated in a toilet, bathed himself, and kept a job. In Martin's mind, however, such a slight deviance was the more appalling for its proximity to the norm. He had turned the light off in his office, and shut the door. In this setting, he could almost tell himself that the phone conversation would never really happen, that he could say anything, anything, whatever conciliatory thing was necessary to end it, to fulfill his obligation and hang up the phone. Talking to Ellen's mother was a nightmare in itself, but talking to Ellen's father could only be faced in the surreality of artificial dusk.

Then, in this quiet haven, Martin had his vision again. In the vision as before, Martin stood on the grocery store sign, but this time he was wearing a flowing white robe. Never in his life had Martin worn anything that could be described as flowing. Not even rippling. In fact, he habitually tucked his t-shirts into his underpants. Yet there he stood on the sign, robe flowing, his short dark haircut sticking up incongruously from billowing yards of that unidentifiable fabric—fleece? muslin?—that is usually identified intuitively as good. The horror that Martin felt at seeing himself thus arrayed was sufficient to shock himself back into his office.

His office was still his office. Toledo was still Toledo. He didn't even feel disoriented nor had there been any sort of sickening transition through waves of distortion or a colored tunnel. Given all this, Martin had to wonder whether the vision had even been real, or if it had been all his fault, blaspheming away again, like an upstart, like a heretic. Martin felt harassed. There is nothing like having a messianic vision when you are about to suffer through a phone conversation with your girlfriend's retard dad.

Martin picked up the phone and dialed the number, taking a deep breath and planting his feet firmly under his desk, laying his free hand flat on its surface, relaxing his eyebrows, and making a shallow calm. Maybe the mother would answer.

"Hello?" said Ellen's father.

"Hello," said Martin. "This is Martin."

"Martin!" said Ellen's father. "Hello! How are you?"

"I'm fine, sir," said Martin, producing a nice smile in the dark of his office. Kind to retarded fathers. Responsible about delivering news. On the other hand, irresponsible about guarding girlfriends. Blasphemer like you wouldn't believe. This guy Martin is a mixed bag.

"It's been a while since we've seen you kids. Mother was just talking about you this morning."

"I thought you'd be…Well…How's everything at the farm?"

"I have the day off!" Ellen's father said. "Early foals coming lately I've been working through nights of course."

"I…um…"

"How's Ellen? I was thinking she could come home soon, see them. She was always so scared—of the little ones!" Ellen's father laughed. "But maybe not any more? She should come and see them anyway!"

"She's not here, actually."

"Well, she could come down for the weekend, I have to work most of this weekend of course, but she and Mother could come down and…"

This is what they always talked about. When the next visit would be possible. What would happen during the next visit. Even if Martin wasn't coming. He would drive her halfway there in his car, and Ellen's father would meet them at an exit off the freeway, and they would transfer the girl between them, and retransfer after. Ellen always smelled a little different when she got back in his car, but Martin stopped smelling it after a few minutes. Ellen's parents still lived in the house she had grown up in. Her father still worked on the same farm. Her mother still sat in the same chairs, slept in the same bed. Her brother was a car mechanic. For Martin, on some level, this was astonishing and enviable. To move in the same lines in which one has always moved, to work, to home, and back. Never mind that the father was damaged and the mother was aggressive. The system, viewed from afar, was beautiful. The gap between them, somehow horrifying. The father had been talking, and now said that they had a new cable company, and were finally able to see real court cases on television, not just fake courtroom shows.

"I'm actually calling, sir…that's…because Ellen is missing."

When he had said the words he felt their shape come out of the whirling mist he had been living in since she'd gone, and he felt that it was absolutely true. She was missing. There was some silence on the line as Martin thought of what to say about it.

"The police have been notified, of course, and we are doing what we can to find her. I don't want you to worry, but I thought you should know, so that you and Mrs. Noll…can just know…what's going on."

"Missing?" Ellen's father's voice was panicky and confused.

"Yes," Martin gritted his teeth together. "She's been missing for five days now actually. I didn't want to worry you before I knew that she was really gone."

And now he knew that? He couldn't know that. It was too easy to keep on doing things to bring her back. And keep running the business. He had said, "Let's keep running the business, because it's all we can do," and Stef had said, "Yes, yes, let's run the fucking business. Let's run the fucking business until we puke. Run, run, run."

"Is she dead?"

"No, sir, she's not dead, she's just…we're not sure where she is."

"How is she missing? It could be that she just left for a trip. Maybe she didn't tell you, because maybe she was coming home for a trip. Maybe she will be here soon."

"I don't think so, sir," Martin felt like he was probably going to jump through the phone line and murder this man, or else go there, fall into his arms and just die. His teeth were grinding against each other, and he had a headache. If he were actually wearing that robe, he thought, throwing caution to the wind, he'd give it a good old-fashioned rend. Impossible to rend tight black t-shirts. Martin tried to imagine himself in sackcloth and ashes. But there was his haircut, ruining everything.

"How did she get missing? Where did she go?"

Martin thought of Ellen's father sitting in their house, sitting on one of the darkly upholstered chairs that was covered in fabric pills. His boots would be dirty on the scuffed and ancient hardwood floor, and he would grip the phone in his hand, pulling the phone wire that coiled and stretched from the wall unit in the kitchen. His smooth forehead was never crossed with wrinkles. His arms were thick with muscles, and his broad torso was fat and tight. He would be hunched, one elbow leaning on the side of the chair, and the phone pressed tightly to his head so he could hear clearly. His eyes would be wide open, staring. Martin felt sorry for himself and for this man, for two men who were talking on the phone to each other under such difficult circumstances.

"She was sitting in the car, and I went into a store. When I came out, the car was gone and she was gone. I haven't heard from her since."

"Kidnapped?" said Ellen's father. "Was she kidnapped?"

"I don't know what happened," said Martin, "but I think she was kidnapped because I don't think she would have just gone."

"No," said Ellen's father firmly, "She wouldn't have just gone. She wouldn't have gone."

"Because where would she have gone?" asked Martin, feeling relieved. "Where would she go? If she went home, she would be there by now. If she went to visit Tracy, because they found the car in Cinncinnati, then Tracy would know it, but Tracy doesn't. So where did she go? Someone took the car. Someone took the car, because I left the keys in it when I went into the store."

Martin was breathing heavily and he felt like he might want to lie down. He felt a migraine coming, but there were no more lights to turn off, and he didn't want to get off the phone. Ellen's father was listening to him, and agreeing with him. Ellen couldn't have just gone. But which possibility was more frightening? Left or kidnapped? Fake visions or real?

"She was kidnapped," said Ellen's father. "Someone kidnapped her in the car from outside the store where it was parked."

"Yes," said Martin. "That's what happened."

"I have to tell Mother," said Ellen's father, "I have to go."

"I don't know what to do," said Martin. Martin imagined Ellen's father hanging up the phone and going upstairs and sitting down on the bed next to his wife, who would talk quietly to him, and maybe hold his head in her lap. Probably this man would cry, and then get up onto his feet after crying. The wife would look tired and sad, and then they would go to bed, and wake up. The father would go to work, and they would be missing a daughter that wasn't really part of everyday life. Nothing that they would really see every day anyway. Here in the city, Martin was walking around in a daze, trying to figure out how it happened, and trying to talk to the police. Trying to do everything right, without Ellen, was impossible, because Ellen was constantly there every day, but was not here now.

"I have to go," repeated Ellen's father. "You can call us. You call us tomorrow."

Yes, he would call them tomorrow. He would tell them how things were progressing.

"Alright."

"Maybe she will show up here at home. Then we will call you."

"Alright."

The phone went dead. When he heard the dial tone, he knew that Ellen's father had hung up. He clicked the phone off and set it down on the desk. Outside in the bar, the party raged. It had been Jane's idea. No, it had been Stef's idea. Jane had been sitting on the barstool, and Ellen had not been sitting on the barstool. Therefore, Jane was there as a girl, and not as a cop. Martin had given a martini, three olives, to the girl on the barstool. He slid the martini over with a perfect meniscus. Any one more drop would bubble on the top, probably bounce right back off. It was all correct, the way a martini should be.

Jane took a swig. "Ever heard of vermouth?" she asked.

Martin chose not to hear it, and hovered over to the sink where he stacked up glasses out of the drying tray. Stef sat on his stool, making a show of looking outside for people who might be coming in. It seemed very silent to Martin, more silent than 4 o'clock had ever been on any other day.

"I know," said Jane. "We could make signs."

"Signs?" said Martin.

"Signs," she went on, "to hang up at the 7-Eleven. I mean, someone must have seen something."

"The police have questioned the cashiers," Martin told her.

"Yes I know that," she said. "I know that we have questioned the cashiers. But there must have been someone standing around, hanging out on the sidewalk, or, you know, a regular customer that the police didn't question. If the car peeled out of the parking lot like you say, someone might remember what kind of person was driving—if it was a girl or a man, you know."

"Well," said Martin, "Alright. Would that be alright, Stef? We could make signs and hang them around. With tape. Or spray glue."

"Like for a cat," said Jane, "that's run away."

"Or like for a little girl," said Stef, "on a milk carton."

"Exactly," said Martin.

Jane took off her leather jacket and underneath she had on a tight sweater, crisscrossed in a low-cut shape across her breasts. Martin believed she was a C cup. This was, to Martin, notable on a girl who was so very small. Her breasts made her look taller, to him. Also, her thighs were shapely, and her wash of curly hair was quite controlled in its tidy bun.

"Well, what should it say?" said Jane. "Obviously, it's important."

"Should there be a reward?" asked Martin.

Stef grabbed his forehead with his hand and growled, "No there is no reward."

"For information," Martin explained, "I think there should be. Not a reward for, for her return. A reward for information."

"Of course," said Jane. "There's always a reward for information. Otherwise who cares?"

Jane sipped at her drink as if it were a little disgusting.

"Eat the olives," Martin told her. She should have eaten up the olives, dipping them in the liquid and pulling them off the toothpick slowly, bit by bit, chewing them and dipping them back in. But she had not done that, exactly. She had not eaten the olives at all.

Stef had said that the reward should be free drinks at the club for one night, and Martin had devised a system where everyone who showed up to respond to the flier would have to be questioned first by Jane, who would then stamp their hands, and then they could drink for free all night. They would have to testify first, of course, or they would be too drunk, or they might just leave. Stef's friend who always made the fliers made a flier. It had turned out looking more like an ad for a rave than like a police flier, but the turn-out had been impressive. Jane was out there at a little table, taking down descriptions. The thick music pulsing through the building reached Martin's dark office and made him want to throw up. He forced himself to stand up and walk out through the dark back room, and he swung open the door into the club. Jane's eyes immediately rose to meet his, and Stef's did too from the door where he was standing.

Martin tried to be a good party host, moving around the room and speaking to this or that person. However, he didn't know anyone there really—they'd closed the club to regulars for this "Private Party." People wanted to talk to him about Ellen, not realizing that he was the boyfriend who had "left that poor chick all alone in the car," and while he didn't feel the need to explain, he also didn't want to appear callous. Stef had been urging him to say something, make a speech, because it looked like he didn't care or notice that Ellen was gone. Stef didn't like Jane hanging around. Jane didn't like Stef either. It was a confusing irksome drama. Jane said she could understand why Martin was staying calm, because it was after all he who had been wounded. It was his car that was stolen, his errant girlfriend on the loose. Of course he would not be grieving—ludicrous thought! Stef said he was acting like an automaton, and that he should let his true feelings show, and stop "running around town" with Jane, who wasn't a "professional."

To Martin, the disappearance of Ellen was an equation with too many variables. It was impossible to solve for X while M and N were squabbling over who was the numerator and who the denominator. The true relationships were unknown, missing. All Martin wanted to do was divide by a final zero and end the whole thing. But to truly finally end it by throwing himself off the grocery store sign was absolutely impossible with Ellen gone. With his universe in such impressive disarray he did not feel like being at a party.

Because who even knew if he was a messiah or not? Can't go around dying for people who have been kidnapped and killed.

He drifted around through unfamiliar faces and ended behind Jane's chair. She pushed back in her seat and looked at him upside down, showing all of her white neck and making her sharp chin into a peak.

"Are you getting anything interesting?" Martin asked, resisting the urge to pat his hand along the side of her face and feel if it was warm and soft. It looked to be both, and he wanted to touch her.

"No," she stretched, closing her eyes and shoving her little fists out to the side. He could have picked her up easily by each outstretched arm, until she dropped them, shook her head, and rubbed her eyes.

"Well, shit," said Martin. "Nothing?"

Jane straightened up, with him behind her. She shuffled the papers on the table around and then sat still, crunching her elbows into her sides.

"Let's get out of here," she said. "I'll tell you what little I did get, and…I just want to get out of here sort of."

Martin offered her his hand. She took it, gripping his fingers.

"Let's go," he said. "I couldn't agree more."

They went out of the club, and Martin nodded to Stef, saying, "We're not getting anything and this is over. Make sure everyone drinks as much as they want. Having said that, cut them off as soon as possible. I'll be back later to close up."

Jane was tugging at his hand, almost out on the sidewalk. Stef stood there rigidly, saying, "Where are you going? With her? Did she interview everyone?"

"It wasn't a good idea," Martin said, quickly. "Nobody remembers anything, she says."

"She does," said Stef. "How very fucking interesting. I'm surprised someone didn't 'remember' that

Ellen flipped off the world, sacrificed a virgin, and sold your car to Satan."

"Look, I'm going," Martin said firmly. "I can't stay here."

Stef yelled after him as he left down the sidewalk with Jane, "What, is it too depressing? What with Ellen gone, and all? Is it getting to you? Hey—let me know what you find out. I'll be here."

Outside everything was better. The fresh air helped his head, and he thought that driving would be pleasant. They got into his car, and he saw Jane push herself down in the seat, letting her head drop below the window.

"That's what Ellen used to do," he said, starting the motor.

"It is?" asked Jane excitedly, shoving herself down more.

"Yes," said Martin, "but her knees used to press up against the dashboard."

Jane put her shoes up on the dash and braced herself back against the seat. "Do you mind?" she said.

"No," he said. "It's nice."

"You know, this is a very unsafe position to be in, should there be a wreck. My legs would be broken. I've seen it."

As they drove out of the parking lot and back past the bar, Jane pointed up to the grocery store sign. "I have always thought, about that sign," she said, "that it would be a good place from which to commit suicide. You could just drop down off the sign and land in the parking lot. I'd probably die, from that height, don't you think? Maybe you wouldn't though. But I would. Maybe you would just be hurt, just lying there on the pavement, but I would die. Some shock for the shoppers!"

Jane giggled. Martin gulped and shivered, gripping the wheel. Probably she was a cop. But possibly she was an agent for whoever was sending the visions.

Not that anyone was sending them. At the very least, at the very most basic, at the very most earnest, solid core, she was a girl sitting in his car where there should be a girl sitting. But Joan of Arc? And suicide? What?

"Where are we going?" he said.

"Let's go to the 7-Eleven."

"You think we might see something there?" asked Martin.

"I think we should go to the 7-Eleven," she repeated, pressing her shoes into the dashboard and her butt into the seat, leaving a mark.

The parking lot of the 7-Eleven looked exactly as it had the night that Ellen disappeared. It was a bright place. Surely someone must have seen something. There were so many people at the party. Surely one of them must have noticed who took Ellen. Martin parked the car and looked at Jane.

"Now what?" he said.

"Now," said Jane, putting her hand over his hand which was on the key chain and ready to turn off the ignition, "You go into the store, and leave the car running. I'll stay here with the radio on."

"What?" said Martin. "What if you get kidnapped?"

He stopped it from sounding how it might have sounded—full of anxiety and concern—and it came out sounding ridiculously casual.

"I won't," said Jane, "and then we'll know that she wasn't kidnapped at all. See? When you come out of that store and see me, sitting here, still in the car, you'll know that she wasn't kidnapped. That she just left."

Martin sat for a moment in the driver's seat, his hand still on the ignition. He looked at her and she was nodding at him encouragingly.

"Just go!" she told him happily. "Nothing will happen, and then we'll just go home!"

"Are you supposed to do this? I mean, is this…like…shouldn't you have backup or something? Isn't this dangerous?"

Jane put one hand on each side of his face in a nice gesture, "There is no danger, Martin. This is just for you. So you can see that she wasn't kidnapped! Just be sure you stay in there a good long time, so you know it's not just because you hurried. Now go!"

She leaned down and turned on the radio, and appeared to be only interested in finding a station. Martin got out of the car and shut the door. Something about this reenactment appealed to him. This time, it would turn out right. He would go into the store, leaving the girl in the car. When he came back out, this time, the girl would still be there with the car, listening to the radio like she should be. He tried to make exactly the same movements he had made the night that Ellen disappeared. He opened the door with his right hand, and made an immediate right hand turn in the store, back to the soft-drink cases. He lingered for a little extra time while choosing a grape juice, so firm was his belief that Jane would still be in the car when he returned. He didn't have to worry. There was a prescribed line of action, and a prescribed result. There was a preordained conclusion, which had misfired the other time, but would now go off perfectly. He stopped, as he remembered he had stopped the other night, in front of the magazine rack, to look for the new *Esquire*. The other night it hadn't been there, but tonight it was. He decided not to buy it, and went up to the counter.

It was so tempting to look out the window just once to see if the car was there. Wouldn't he feel absolutely stupid in the police department twice in one week, reporting a missing woman, and this time a police officer! He would probably become a local legend, but the wrong kind. It was almost physically painful not to look out the window and see the car. But he kept his eyes firmly on the man in front of him, asked him for cigarettes, paid him, and then turned. The car was there. She was sitting in it. He had a hard time not running out the door to get back inside.

When he opened the door and dropped back into the driver's seat, her warmth was gratifying. He handed her the bottle of grape juice.

"Is this for me? Oh, is that what you were getting for her? You poor thing! I'm right here—there was never any need to worry, see? Here I am!"

He half-laughed, and didn't know what to do. She leaned over and hugged him, and when he hugged back it seemed he pulled her right into his lap over the emergency brake, and she came so lightly. She had her arms around him and was real, a real girl very happy with herself, and firm and purposeful. She pulled out of the hug and looked at his face. She looked very pretty close up. As Martin was deciding whether to kiss her mouth, she pulled close and kissed him first. He felt the tingle of a new kiss, the first mouth other than Ellen's mouth in a very long time. It felt like kissing had changed. It was very different. Then she smiled out of it, a very graceful way to leave a kiss he thought, and he saw Stef.

Stef was just outside the door of the 7-Eleven, glaring at him and shaking his head from side to side. Jane couldn't see him, and she laughed, sitting in Martin's lap facing him. She pressed against his body and let her head rest on his shoulder. He put one arm around her waist, looking back at Stef who appeared to be very angry. He had a handful of fliers in his hand, had been tearing them down from the bulletin board inside.

When he was seven, Martin had lost his dog. The dog had been a giant husky, and Martin, who was a very small child, could have ridden the dog. The dog's position was one of infinite tolerance. Martin and the dog acted together the way that a child acts with a deaf mute father who is paralyzed. Once, his mother caught Martin hitting the dog slowly and repeatedly over the head with a brick. Martin was seated in the grass and the dog lay beside him with his eyes squinted, his head close to the ground. His mother, who had been carrying empty jam jars to the garage, dropped the jars on the porch, shattering them, screaming at Martin to stop. She yanked him away from the dog, threw the brick over the fence, and knelt beside the husky, cradling its head in her lap. Later that year, the dog had disappeared. Martin had made a poster with markers that he and his mother had photocopied at the Post Office and nailed to telephone poles in their neighborhood. The dog did not return for weeks. Finally, Martin crawled under the porch to investigate an odor, and found the dog, dead, with a large wound in its chest and blood crusted on its fur. His mother explained, in tears, that maybe the dog had been standing with his legs up on the fence, and the neighbor, who had always threatened to kill the dog with an ice pick, ever since the dog had killed the neighbor's Doberman, had hit him with an ice pick in the chest. Martin had asked why the dog didn't come to them. The mother said he had just crawled under the porch to die. Which didn't answer the question.

Chapter Eight

Molly came twice a day to feed Ellen, let her go to the bathroom, and take her outside for a few minutes. The rest of the time, Ellen was in an upstairs room, with a pile of magazines, a television, and a mattress. The room was locked, and a large bookshelf was shoved up against the door from the outside when Ellen was inside. Molly spoke curtly to her now, and always seemed to be in a big rush. Ellen had expected things to go differently, but it was better than the tunnel. She now knew what had happened to her: Stef was Molly's boyfriend. Molly's boyfriend had kidnapped her. Molly's boyfriend had thought he was doing the right thing. Molly's boyfriend had thought he was supposed to kidnap her. And really, wasn't he? Molly thought yes, and Jay thought no. At least it had been discussed in his presence. Maybe it had been casually mentioned that the only way for Jay was to kidnap a bride. Maybe it had been a standing joke. Maybe one night it had been discussed in detail, over a couple of drinks. Whatever.

The house was located on a peaceful street in what Ellen identified as Swanton, a rather distant and detached "suburb" of Toledo. She felt better being not very far away from Martin and The Joyride and home. But she didn't like being in Swanton. Once long ago, Ellen had been to Swanton. She and her college roommate had been invited by a friend to participate in recording an album for the friend's band, in the friend's studio at the friend's house. After getting off the freeway at Airport Road and driving south through Swanton's main drag, she and her friend began to experience what they thought were strange hallucinations. Every storefront looked artificial. Every house looked exaggerated. A hot dog joint named "Giant Dog" was advertised on an enormous hot dog thirty feet above the ground. Also, there were no people. Ellen had expected carnival music at any moment, or fanged clowns, or a dead child in the middle of the road. It all began to be very horrible and exciting. Their friend's house was way out in the woods. After the recording session was over (during which Ellen and her roommate had been requested to scream and moan into the microphone for six minutes, and that was the extent of it), they'd lounged around the studio while the friend and his band told ghost stories about Swanton. "There were devil dogs between the trees," said the bass player, "that had red eyes!" Ellen and her roommate heard all about the Indian burial grounds, and the Satanists that had been caught last year sacrificing chickens. The band was full of boys. The boys glowed with their freaky narratives. When they had to leave, it was dark, and the girls ran to the car, scrambling for the key, switching on the dome light, laughing, calling their friend crazy, reminding each other that he had once been "locked up" in a "loony bin." Since then, luxury subdivisions had sprung up from what had once been the Black Swamp. Jay's house was in one of these subdivisions, safe, paved, planted with reasonable trees, full of four-door sedans and lawnmowers. Still, it gave her a creepy feeling.

For three days, Ellen watched soap operas and nighttime dramas, read magazines, and stared out the window at the neighbors. The neighbors were engaged in preparing their landscaping for the full onslaught of spring, whenever that should occur. They wore windbreakers and rubber boots, and pulled up old plants, scraped clean the little knobs of dirt that held the bushes, and raked around the edges of sidewalks. The neighbors did a good job with everything. They were thrilled when under the muck of winter they found little crocus plants already emerging. They called each other to come see.

When the neighbors were in the yard, quietly working, concentrating, Ellen considered opening the window and screaming out to them, "Help me! I can't get out of this house! Help me!" but she assumed that the window wouldn't open. Once, when the Daddy neighbor was standing, leaning on his rake, she beat on the window hard with both hands, more to feel her hands beating on the window than to attract attention. If he looked up, she could always duck out of sight. She ducked, just in case. When she looked back out, the Daddy neighbor was looking around, as if confused. Essentially, she did not want him to see her, because upstairs she was hiding in her room.

Maybe if the Daddy neighbor did see her at the window, he thought that she was a sick person, confined to her room because of a terrible disease. He probably thought she had been a poet, or a painter, a very influential artist of her generation, who was now struck with palsy, unable to write or paint, and too mortally depressed to try. She would never leave the house again, just stay in this room with her typewriter and her oils, the very things that had given her so much joy. They would sit there staring at her, mocking her, and she'd stare back, becoming violent, hurting herself loudly until the personal nurse came in and medicated her. She would struggle under the nurse's bored persuasions, but the nurse would never understand, would shoot her full of drugs, and leave her there shaking. She would be under heavy sedatives. The Daddy neighbor would know that she couldn't be expected to speak to him or communicate with him because she was in a daze of tranquilizers, and to her he would appear blurry, bigger, smarter, older.

If he saw her, and he thought she was upset, he might try and contact the police. Because he, typically, would not understand what was really going on. If he contacted the police, and she was rescued, then realistically, she wouldn't ever be kidnapped again, and so she would be safe from kidnapping forever. No one is ever kidnapped twice. She could go home now and forget being kidnapped again for as long as she lived. That would be it. Safe. Over. No doubt the Daddy neighbor would find this to be satisfactory. No doubt this is what he longed for on a daily basis. So she tried to smile out the window, to show that even while suffering, she was keeping her spirits up. No interference was necessary.

Ellen didn't see much of Jay, although sometimes he did come into her room and talk to her, never letting her out, and always locking the door behind him. Molly was the one who let her out. At times, Ellen considered attacking Molly, overpowering her, slapping her around, and demanding to be released. However, she thought that maybe Molly had a knife, or had someone waiting in the car who would chase her down and run her over if she fled, and the fact that this person would probably be Stef didn't convince her to risk it. She had a new respect for Stef. Even though his three days of Mars/Venus synchronicity must now surely be over, she now thought, "I know what he's capable of." He had hit her, and knocked her out. No, she thought, it is best to stay here and not try and get away from Molly. Molly herself seemed threatening enough with her silence and her severe commands, her baby hands making fake-gun whenever she came into the room, her eternal glancing around, her boots. Ellen took a shower every time Molly came to let her out of the room, even if she came three times in one day. The shampoo Molly gave her smelled just like technology. The food Molly gave her was pretty fattening.

On the fourth day, in the afternoon, Ellen heard someone moving the bookshelf away from the door and not having too much trouble moving it. This let her know that Jay was coming in. She sat up on the mattress, put the magazine down, and poked her legs out in front of her. She tried not to look at the door. She tried to look pensive. The door opened and Jay stood there, smiling at her.

"I'm moving in today," he said. "Do you want to come downstairs?"

Later, Ellen rattled the chain on her handcuffs against the banister in the big house that was empty except for everything that Jay was bringing in. The house was probably gorgeous and certainly new, but there were dust cloths thrown over the floors and wrapped around chandeliers and across fireplaces. Bright light flooded the foyer where Ellen was caught half bent over, so the only way she could really be comfortable was to sit on the stairs and let her hands hang from the cuffs. Jay wore pressed denim coveralls and clean boots. He carried every box and package with both hands. Ellen felt like she was watching tennis, or a car race: back and forth, around and around through the foyer to the kitchen around the dining room to the big parlor and then out. Sometimes, he stopped to show Ellen a kitchen tool, or a pillow, holding it up to her and explaining, for example, "This is used in bed to cradle your head while you sleep. It is shaped like a rectangle because that way, when there are two placed side by side at the head of the bed, they fit exactly. Because it is made out of down, it is typically covered by a cloth case, so that the case can be washed periodically, and the pillow itself does not get dirty. Of course, we take baths before using the pillow, so the case does not get very dirty either. Therefore, the important secondary function of the case is to change the color of the pillow so that it matches the different sets of sheets, dust ruffles, bedspreads, and comforters."

Looking around the house, Ellen was reminded of the homes of several high-school friends, who had invited her over on occasion. It had the same bigness, the same austerity. Ellen thought about what kind of wardrobe she would have to acquire, were she to continue living here. Matching things. Pastels. Multiple sets of accessories. She thought that even her play clothes would have to match—peach jumpsuits, lemon-yellow sweatpants with a hooded jacket and a white t-shirt. She thought she would rather continue wearing dresses. After each item that Jay held up to her, Ellen nodded and smiled. She knew he was trying to be funny, but she had learned that most of the things she said upset him, so she kept quiet. Ellen wore a too-small t-shirt of Molly's, and a too-small cardigan, over a too-small skirt which was pinned into place because the buttons didn't reach, with too-small tights which kept on falling down. Her long body felt pinched and irritated. She sat on the stairs in the house where Jay was bringing in his possessions, moving in, and thought about Martin, and how Stef was a betrayer, and how now she would never be able to go back, because everything was thwarted, and would have to change, and change, and change.

Jay pushed the front door open with his back, came backwards through it, and then kept it open with his right elbow while he pulled in a large TV in a big TV box.

"This is my new television," he said.

"Do you want me to help you with that?"

"No, I don't think so," said Jay, as he let the door swing shut behind him. He let the box rest on the floor in the foyer, leaning on it with both hands. "I don't think I want to take your handcuffs off because you might try and run for it."

When he spoke about her being kidnapped, his eyes widened on purpose, as if he were telling a wild story to a small child. Like when you say, "Then the MONSTER came and TICKLED THE LITTLE BOY TO DEATH!" This made Ellen think the whole thing was a joke, something he did for entertainment, as if he were filling in blanks that he saw with conversation. She found his performance ultimately unsatisfying. However he seemed in some ways so earnest, as if putting on a big fake act and hoping that someone in the crowd would believe it to be true, so that he could not be held accountable, and yet the message would be heard. In some ways, she wanted him to pull a gun on her, but in other ways, she thought it was very funny that he did not, and wanted him to laugh about it too. She felt compelled to make him laugh, in sync with her laughing, so that he would not be hurt about it, so that he would have a good time.

"I wouldn't try and run for it," she said.

"Well, if you did try, your stockings would fall down around your ankles."

Ellen laughed, "Yes, they would."

"That is all part of my ingenious plan," he said, still leaning on the television, "to put you into my sister's stockings. Much more crucial even than the handcuffs which prior to this very important task of keeping you chained to my staircase were relegated only to duties attached to her minor and very infrequent incidences of sexual experimentation."

She smiled at him.

"I would like," he said, "to have a house warming party."

"Well you can't wear that."

"Allow me to say, woo hoo."

Ellen laughed. She felt like maybe if Jay threw a housewarming party, then it would be a big event. There would be many, many party guests, people she had never met before. Maybe one of them would be someone she vaguely knew or had met once, and that person would say, "Aren't you Ellen Noll?" and she would say, "What?" and move along through the room. She had spent three days living in this house, by herself mostly, locked up in a room, with Molly coming over infrequently to provide food and water and bathroom trips. She didn't like going to the bathroom twice a day—once in the morning before Molly went to class, and then once in the evening before Molly went out. It was uncomfortable, and boring, and confusing. She couldn't figure out if her real kidnapper was Molly or Jay. Of course, when Jay had shown up today ready to move in, she'd been elated, for whatever reason there was. She almost wished she had a job, so she could be missing work. She wished she had plans, so she could be ruining them. She missed Martin. Molly refused to engage in conversation.

Jay picked up the television and carried it into the parlor.

"This is where we'll watch television together after I get back from the office each night. We will watch the eleven o'clock news and then later we will comment on each day's events to each other as we get ready for bed."

Ellen looked up at him and raised her eyebrows, but he was earnestly removing the TV from its box. It was so hard, because just when she thought he was being absolutely cynical, he turned up wounded.

"Sure, then we can turn off both our lamps and pull up the covers," she said, "just like Lucy and Ricky."

He turned to face her, "Just like Lucy and Ricky, with one notable exception."

"Of course," she said. "No striped pajamas."

"Of course."

Maybe there was a party atmosphere already, layered through with his palpable tension, and her fatigue. Maybe they would only have to invite some friends, and a party would rage until dawn. She wondered what his friends were like. Maybe they were all fascinatingly insane. They sat on the moment for a few minutes, and then she asked him if he had any money.

"What do you mean?"

"Well, what do you do for a job? Do you work at that place with the tunnel?"

"Yes and no," he said. "At the same time yes and at the same time no. I work there, yes, but I do not work there as I am supposed to work there. I am supposed to be upstairs in an office, right now, at this second, and yet, I am not there, nor have I ever been into my office, nor have I ever accepted the title of Junior Vice President of Strategic Planning."

"Why not?"

"My father…," Jay began, and then broke off and pulled at the straps on his coveralls, laughing, "Ah, I do not look the part! Do you want to go shopping? I believe I need a brand-new sofa!"

"Alright," said Ellen, "but what if someone sees you and me together? I could be rescued. I'm sure the police are looking for me. What about that?"

"Well, I will have to torture you until you tell me the location of a mall at which we are not likely to be noticed. Would you like me to commence torturing now? Or should we perhaps move into the bathroom where your blood will not stain my impressive foyer, and your removed digits can be tossed directly into the toilet for untraceable flushing?"

Jay moved toward her menacingly, and then fell upon her, tickling her ribcage with mad fervor. Ellen's butt slid off the step she was sitting on, and she hung by her hands from the banister, laughing and saying, "Ouch ouch." He continued to tickle her clumsily, and was hurting her, and she looked up into his face and saw that he was scared, and that the effort to be jovial was undoing him. So she let him tickle her, feeling his hands and his hard proximity, and watching his nervousness. He was smiling with perfect teeth, and seemed so like a rich-boy underwear model. His manner didn't fit. She felt fairly certain he had terrible mental problems. She wondered if being kidnapped was guaranteed to make her more or less prejudiced against criminals. She wondered if it would make her a wise person, or a good person, or if she would emerge from it with terrible paranoias that could never be cured. No matter how much she thought that he was a criminal, she still liked being close to him, and liked feeling his body up against her when he tickled her. He felt warmer than Martin, softer, more pliable. In that moment she wanted to undress him, bring him to an orgasm, and make him happy. Maybe he had a way to wipe out her memory. Maybe he had advanced brainwashing techniques. Maybe the brainwashing would begin any second, and she would feel nothing, nothing from her life with Martin, nothing to stop her from pulling him inside her and being happy. Martin would find her eventually. She knew this. Meanwhile, she could be very brave. She could be wise. She met Jay's gaze and tried to exude confidence and charisma. Here was someone on whom an impression could be made.

"Bowling Green!" she said finally, trying to pull herself back up with her fingers on the banister. "Let's go there!"

They arrived at the mall and Jay took her elbow tightly in his grip to pull her along into the building.

She saw a woman's eyes following her with curiosity, perhaps jealousy, certainly keen interest. She stood up straight and shook her elbow a little bit, trying to loosen his grip. Was this where she should scream, make a scene, disrupt his plan? There was a security guard by the door. Should she plant her feet right now on this dark pavement and start wailing that she was here against her will, that the man she was with was a stranger, that she belonged somewhere far away? Before she could decide how best to do it, or when, they were inside the doors and her feet were tapping on tile.

At the department store, Jay was meticulous in his examination of the merchandise. In every section of the store, Jay picked up items, handled them carefully, remarked on their good or bad qualities, and then replaced them. Ellen was most concerned about why no one noticed her handcuffs, or the way she and Jay proceeded exactly together through the store, never separating to look at different displays, always right together, as he had his hand firmly clamped around her elbow. She was handcuffed! She tried to let the cuffs dangle far down around her wrists, beneath the cuffs of the long coat she had been given to wear. Jay appeared to be having a good time. He suggested that they not only buy a couch but also new clothes for Ellen. She would have to tell him her size, because she couldn't try them on. She couldn't be alone, by herself in the dressing room. She told him she didn't want new clothes, so he estimated her size and bought them anyway. Standing at the register, Ellen made intense eyes at the cashier, telegraphing her state of kidnap, and her longing to be rescued, and her profound disinterest in new fashions. The cashier didn't pick up on anything! She looked at Ellen and Jay as if she thought they were a very attractive couple. She looked affirming and positive and as if she were saying, "Yes!" From this Ellen understood that the cause was lost, and that it was best to try and enjoy herself. After all, she had done all she could. She had dropped her coat in the elevator. She had made gestures at the cashier.

Looking at the clothes Jay picked out for her, Ellen saw that they were the kind of thing an executive would wear, or a smart executive's wife. He bought her a black bag. He bought her shoes. They had bags to carry.

"I thought you were going to buy a couch," she said.

"No, that was a lie," said Jay, weighted down with parcels, but still attempting buoyancy. "I wanted you to have a nice outfit."

"Do you want me to wear these clothes?"

"Yes! To the house-warming party. Molly assures me it will be a tremendous amount of fun."

She found it odd that she was having a normal shopping experience in the middle of this kidnapping, and then thought that the shopping experience was not at all normal. It's just that she was using her same voice for this conversation that she used for others that were more normal. She expected everything to be different, but it wasn't. Her feet hurt. She was tired. It was the same as any other day at four. Except that she wasn't home, and she was very excited and nervous, and something very incredible and strange was happening to her and she was here in the Woodland Mall with the strange man who was buying her outfits.

Jay looked hunted, manic, uncertain, and Ellen wanted to touch him, assure him, make it all okay. This was the wrong place for him, she thought, cheap shopping mall and shitty floor tile. Here is a man in history, she thought, looking at him and his jaw-line and his deep terrible eyes of confusion, and here he stands buying me an outfit in a mall I don't even like! She felt intimidated by Jay, because in this new drama of her life, he played such an important role. So much depended on him. She was not intimidated by Jay because of the

money he had. This, to her, was all part of the enter-
prise. She felt she had to be careful with him, and do
things to him, so that it would play right, so that things
would happen correctly. What if she were to piss him
off, and he became idiotic, angry, or disinterested?
What was her reaction to this outfit supposed to be?
She decided that to be overly happy would ruin his
attempts to please her. Also, she was kidnapped, so
she had to be miserable. She thought that because he
had bought her a week's worth of clothes, that he intended to keep her for at least another week. So, in this
way, it was progressing. There would be a party. She
would be handcuffed, or not. She would be a success,
or not. There would be guests, drinks, a social atmosphere. She could slip away and, unnoticed, escape! In
tatters she would arrive at The Joyride, open the door,
fall into Martin's arms, prosecute, testify, show no re-
morse!

Jay waited for her by the entrance to the mall while
she took a drink from a water fountain. It was the far-
thest they had been from each other all day.

Chapter Nine

Ellen stood on the street outside the party. She wore a brown skirt, long down to her ankles, with a slit to the knee. She wore no stockings. She wore brown leather shoes, thick and strappy, with a steep heel. She wore a black knit top with long sleeves and a V-neck that stretched tight around her long waist. Her hair was smoothed down around her face and hung at her collarbones in limp acquiescence, mastered by a potion the lady at the spa had given her. Her makeup was dull, a tricky matte. She wore a heavy choker of dense dark metal. She looked different than she had ever looked—richer, and less real. Looking at herself in the mirror she had been surprised. Ellen began to walk, away from the house, down the sidewalk with the same placid gait she'd used to walk out the door. She was getting a breath of fresh air. She passed two houses, and then three. She reached the stop sign and crossed the street.

Since the shopping trip, Ellen had lived in Jay's house for a week, and he had visited her each day, taking her out to restaurants, or to get her hair done, or to see a movie. During each visit he had been absently polite, exactly attentive, and cryptic. He treated her like an exotic pet, or an esteemed visitor. Sometimes Ellen tried to be clever, or smart, or make him laugh, but it never came off quite right, and she often saw him smile forcedly, or sigh. Every time she tried to rise to the occasion, she tripped up, or if she got off a good line he hadn't been listening, or if she put on a funny face he had just looked away. She knew he was amazingly smart. She knew that her main claim to greatness was that she had been picked, chosen, kidnapped. That is why he treated her so well, and bought her things, and attempted to make her comfortable. She thought he was constantly confused, and hadn't had time to sort everything out, or didn't want to. She often felt him pushing things along, as she herself was inclined to do, toward the next step, without thinking or analyzing.

They had arranged the house together, not talking much about the future except in terms of jokes or hyperbole, and the house looked beautiful and perfect. Ellen's room was now fully finished, including pictures on the wall and a mirrored vanity which Jay had outfitted himself with perfumes, cosmetics, powders, and a wooden hairbrush. She watched him do everything from her captive position, handcuffed to whatever thing was handy, and then locked into the room each night with the bookshelf. During all this time she had been mostly silent, unimpressed with her own efforts at dazzle, and unwilling to upset him with more. Each night, after he left, she thought to herself that she was essentially a boring person.

On the day of the party, Molly arrived instead of Jay, and told Ellen to take a shower. While Ellen was in the shower, Molly sat on the toilet with the lid down.

"You're going to meet our parents today," said Molly, in a subdued voice. "They're going to be at the party."

"Oh really?" asked Ellen. Ellen felt older than Molly. She felt like Molly was an aberrant teenager and couldn't be held responsible. She also felt like Molly was very likable and cute, and that if Molly had been kidnapped, Molly would have endeared herself to everyone by now. Ellen had always believed that a true kidnapped person could work charms on her kidnappers that her kidnappers could ill ignore. She hoped to be that sort of kidnapped person, but was unsure where to begin.

"Yes really. You're going to meet Mom and Dad Harrey."

"Mmm," said Ellen, squirting shampoo into her hand. "Are you going to introduce me in chains? This is our captive Ellen? Shake hands but do not rattle her, ha ha?"

"No, you're going to be out of your handcuffs," said Molly.

Ellen thought about this.

"You're Jay's fiancée," said Molly. "The only thing they're going to be thinking about is the impropriety of you living together before the wedding."

"I'm not going to have handcuffs on?"

"You know," said Molly, slouching down, "there was supposed to be brainwashing, I guess. I was supposed to really change your mind about things, but I didn't have as much time as I thought I would have, and there was a lot going on at school with midterms and everything. You were supposed to be good and brainwashed by the time this party came along. I told Jay I could handle it. I mean, by now, you were supposed to be loose in the house."

"But you didn't have time to brainwash me?"

"Well, it seemed hard," Molly sagged on the toilet, her chin in her hand, the picture of dejection. "Now you'll probably run off the minute your cuffs come off, and that'll be the end of it."

She seemed so different from the day she'd come to take Ellen from the tunnel. Ellen watched her through the shower curtain as she rinsed her hair. So she *was* supposed to be brainwashed. She wondered if she was susceptible to brainwashing, and how they had planned it. Maybe Molly was supposed to tape her eyes open every day for three hours and shout into her face that Jay was beautiful and good, and that her real name was April, and that she had lived in Wisconsin all her life. Maybe she was supposed to have devised a sensory deprivation chamber, where electrodes piped in images of sweet foods and life with Jay. If only the kidnapping had been more organized. But then, thought Ellen, I would have been brainwashed. And it's got to be better not to be brainwashed.

"Well why don't I tell you what I know," she suggested to Molly, "and you can fill me in on the details."

Molly looked up at her and raised her eyebrows, "That's stupid."

Ellen stared straight ahead with the water running over her and cleverly tricked Molly. "Look, we both want the party to be a success, and I don't want Jay to be mad at you. It'll be fine. I'm probably half brain-washed already, and you don't even know it!"

Molly sighed, and rested her head on the toilet tank.

"Okay," she said. "After all it hardly matters. If you're horrible, and run away, it won't be my fault. We can say you got nervous and freaked, or that you discovered Jay was a fruitcake. That would be believable."

Ellen was irritated, as if this apathy and information was going to hinder her alleged brainwashing. Maybe if she wasn't brainwashed, she couldn't go to the party. Then there would be no choice in the matter, just the room again, and more TV.

"Well here's how I see it," she said hurriedly, "Jay's not successful with women, because of his eccentricity, and his habits, you know. He's not exactly completely easy to get along with. He gets a lot of interest, but then when the women spend some time with him, they decide he's not going to be their perfect little golden boy husband, which is, ironically, exactly what he has always wanted to be, which is why he was dating that type of girl in the first place, rather than some computer girl who might have understood him. Am I right? And then there is your father, who wants him to be VP of the company."

"My dad is Jason Harrey."

"Okay."

"Harrey Communications? Telephony?"

"Telephoney?"

"No third E," said Molly automatically, "Alright never mind. It's just a multinational. Nothing you would have ever heard of. Dad wants Jay to be VP of Strategy or Hostile Mergers or Baloney Manufacturing or something."

"Strategic Planning," Ellen said, squeezing the water out of her hair to prepare for a final rinse.

"Right, how did you know that?"

"Brainwashing," said Ellen.

"Fine, whatever."

"Your dad wants Jay to step up and be Junior Executive Sir with a tie and a suburb and a wife and a Mercedes. But— "

"But Jay only wants to be an Airborne Ranger? Listen, you fucking naked strumpet," Molly almost laughed, "Jay wants to be a CEO, but he is more likely, on any given day, to creep down into that ugly pit of software developers and spend sixteen hours straight in front of a monitor goozling out code. See? And instead of the wife and suburb and all that shit, he lives in a downtown loft, drinks Coke, and plays online chess with some geekboy in Norway."

"But he wants to be a CEO?"

"Yes. He goes down in that fucking tunnel and meditates about it. One time he had me role-play so he could practice having an assistant. He sucked at it."

"This may be an inappropriate question for someone in handcuffs, but since I am going to be free in a few hours, I will now ask, what's in it for me?"

Molly sat up, leaned over, and started picking at her boot.

"You'll be rich of course," she said. "Isn't that what all you people want? To be rich?"

Ellen stiffened and then unstiffened and smiled, turning the water off and reaching for her towel.

"Well, sometimes, besides wealth and power, 'we people' do crave privacy. Do you think in your infinite grace and tact, you could grant this simple girl that one simple wish?"

Molly rose from the toilet, sneered, laughed, and left the room.

At the party, Ellen had been very quiet. She had not met Jay and Molly's parents, nor had she met anyone who had not directly accosted her. She was busy wearing her outfit and walking around in her shoes. She was immediately concerned with getting out of the house and walking away. And then she was out, and on her way down the street, and there she was, three blocks away, and no one had come chasing after, and no one had yelled, "Stop her! She's escaping!"

As Ellen walked through the night, she thought of what Jay would say when he found out she had gone. He would probably say, "This is disconcerting, and certainly could have been avoided." Maybe he would say, "That sweet dear girl, how will I ever recover from this loss," or, "That charming vivacious spirit! She will be sorely missed!" Ellen wished she could be there when Jay looked around the room and was crestfallen, or distraught, or enraged. Perhaps he would be angry with her for leaving, and would track her down, scour the city, stop at nothing. Perhaps he would show real terror on discovering that she was missing, and shoot out of the house, looking everywhere for her.

She walked, a little cold now, toward a stoplight, toward Airport Highway. She was really pretty far from the house now, and couldn't see it. She stopped. If Jay were to think back on her, to think back on their time together, what would he remember? Would he remember her being hesitant? Pensive? Fearful? Quiet? She had not so very many chances, and here was her chance, after all, and she had been hesitant. She hadn't wanted to leap in, make the definitions, be something. She'd waited. It disgusted her to think of pulling herself leg by leg to Airport Highway, to a telephone, to waiting in the cold, to sleeping (probably) in Martin's car, to discussions and cold glances. It disgusted her when she thought of Jay, looking at her memory, and thinking in his confused way that she had not been everything he'd hoped, that it had worked out for the best, that she had left at just the right moment.

She remembered a time when her parents' little house had been covered with snow. Outside, her father was using his old rough hands. He was tossing firewood into the basement window, which was open, and down there Mother stacked the wood away from the lamps, away from the carpet, on the stairwell side of the room. Father was battered by wind, and Mother bustled back and forth from the window to her growing pile. Mother had got the idea in her head that the snow would ruin the wood, that the wood would be wet, unusable, and no fire during Ellen's visit. So the two parents had begun to manage it together, with gusts whistling in through the window, and Father's fleecy earflaps blowing up straight. In their shuffling, they had a rhythm, in which Mother was always faster, and waiting, because Father was leaning against the wind, and keeping his coat on, had to select which log to bring next. His eyes teared and he sniffled. Mother stooped to adjust a lampshade, and Father hoisted a log down onto the floor, possibly gouging the linoleum or leaving a mark of moisture.

With Ellen at her elbow, Mother could leave a local craft show withering behind her. She was like Martin in her dryness. Daddy on the other hand could never say bad things, because he either couldn't think of them or because he was too nice. Ellen knew that whenever she couldn't think of a withering thing to say, it wasn't because she was too nice. Therefore it had to be that her Father, and she, had the same problem. The problem was that he was mentally retarded. So if they had the same problem, that meant that she was mentally retarded too. On the street, on the night of the party to open Jay's new house, Ellen was not thinking about this, not even when she remembered her father stumbling around in the snow. But it was there in her brain because it was always there in her brain, along with the panic and the worry and fear and the trapped feelings and thinking she was boring. Ever so slightly, ever so imperceptibly, people must discover, people must perceive, that she was, as he was, slow in the head. It had to be obvious. In the root of her, she knew this.

On that night, in the snowstorm, Mother had looked up to see another block of wood falling into the basement, nearly crushing a small table.

"Henry, don't throw for a second. Hold up," she leaned over piled-up magazines to pull the table farther away from the window. She pulled it towards her and it fell over.

"Henry," she screamed, turning to direct her screaming at the open window, "Stop throwing wood down! I'm just moving things around for a second!"

He could really never hear anything out of his right ear, and with the wind, it was useless to holler at him. He kept flinging wood into the basement and crushed a lamp. He seemed to have forgotten to wait for her to reach. Maybe he wanted to get done with the job or maybe he just forgot. She had pushed everything around again, trying to get organized. Then she got angry, and squeezing her little waist with both hands, she balled her sweater into two knots at the sides. Ellen, on the stairs, wanted to help her, but also wanted to run upstairs and help her father. This is what my parents are doing when I am not here, she thought. They are hating each other because he is stupid.

"Stop it!" Mother shrieked, her tight face in a raging spasm. "I told you to stop throwing down wood!"

At that moment, years ago, Ellen planned to make a phone call. She planned to take her father to visit an old friend so that they could get out of the house for a while. She had planned, on the stairs, that she would take Father away with her forever. Maybe she would never tell where they had gone. Maybe she would tell Mother to go and hang herself from a fire escape right down in the heart of the city of Toledo, where Mother had never been. Most of Ellen's friends in high school said that Ellen's mother was a perfect mother, and wanted to call her Mom, and wanted to stay over.

Ellen watched her mother's fingers reach up the basement wall to get a grip and climb up there so that the next log struck her in the face. She cried out like an animal with blood in its eyes and climbed up, reaching out the window frame. One more log—he was just hefting them blindly—and she took it on the shoulder before she was out the window, pushing herself into the wind outside with the ball of her foot against the window frame. Ellen could see everything, framed this way in the black night square of the window. Staggering erect Mother picked up a log and hurled it at his bent up form. She must have been angry with him for a lot of things, for being the way he was, for being a stupid shit-shoveler with no way to change his life.

"Murderer!"

The gash on her forehead had leaked blood down to her lips, and her fierce knees and hips battled the air. He turned in time to see the log fall toward him, ducked so that it landed on his neck and rocked him back onto the ground. She was on him, and shaking her head from left to right. He stared, more than shocked, into her eyes all stripped of their superior droop. Her teeth were bared as if she couldn't bite them tight enough together.

Then Mother left him there and rushed into the house, and Ellen scrambled up the stairs to meet her as she came in. They arrived in the living room together, Mother with her hair blown to bits, her sweater torn, and her slippers dirty.

"I'm looking for the gun, the rifle." she says, "Your Father is trying to kill me."

"What are you talking about?" asked Ellen.

"He has gone insane," said Mother. "I need to protect myself. I'm going into the bedroom to search for the gun. If he comes in here, please do not tell him where I have gone."

Then she went into the bedroom, and after a while Ellen could hear the shower. Ellen opened the back door, looking for her Father. From the porch she could see him leaning over the fence of the horse pasture, hanging onto the fence as the wind blew him back from it, squinting. The horses had not turned to him, or approached him. They were standing in a circle, butts out. Ellen thought that they should be taken into the barn. She thought that at that very most important moment, as she stood windblown and snow cold on the porch, that something would happen, someone would die, someone would leave forever, and everything would change. But it did not. Everything continued as it always had. Miraculous that it could, but it did.

Now she stood on the sidewalk and felt desperate. She shook her hands around and cried a little bit. She wondered if anyone saw her standing out here, on this subdivision on-ramp, making a decision. It might rain. It might rain and ruin her hair. She made the decision based on her reality, and the fact that Martin was here and Jay was there, and that she would never be there again, and if she left there with the impression behind her of hesitancy and weakness, she would never be able to think about it with satisfaction. She decided to go back into that party, and be the most fascinating kidnapped person in the history of kidnapping, because, after all, it was her duty to Jay to leave him with good memories, and he would probably never kidnap anyone after this, and she would never get kidnapped again, so this was their only chance. In her life, to recreate herself, there was this one opportunity, and it couldn't be left behind just to step into Martin's car and cry and have everything made okay. Of course, also, there was her responsibility to Jay. And her chance, at this very moment, to change everything, break everything, never ever hear from anyone again, and be new.

Each step on her way back to the party was fraught with resolution and determined purpose. She gripped herself, and made herself think of the person she would have always dreamed of being, but more glamorous, more wry, more absolute, more blasé. When she opened the door to the house, she greeted the room with a radiant smile, and went directly to Jay, who was standing with two people she could only identify as his parents.

The house glittered. Every inch of floor was absolutely clean, without the wear of years or the dust of living. Each item in the house glowed with newness, with perfection, with justified placement, with deserved appreciation. Ellen noticed almost nothing of this. She had watched Jay's careful arrangements, and had thought that he certainly was interested in detail. She may have even wondered if he was an obstructionist, or a collector. Tonight, she saw nothing of the exacting splendor around her. It was only for Jay to muse, and fuss, and pick things up and put them down. For here there was purity, absolution, and personality under the lights.

"Mrs. Harrey?" said Ellen.

"Ah Ellen," said Jay, glancing at her with wide eyes of surprise, "I'm so happy to see you're back from your *walk*."

"Of course, darling," she said, pressing her left side against him and extending her right hand to the lady, his mother. "I just felt a little iffy, you know? But now I'm feeling just splendid."

Jay's mother, an austere woman in her late fifties, smiled at Ellen with the perfect teeth of the ruling class, her face stretching aside in obviously false smoothness. Her hair was decidedly silver and smooth, and her skin was markedly tan and tight. Ellen remembered to open her eyes wide, to keep her head up, but chin down, to speak clearly and with precise, deliberate diction.

"It's lovely to meet you, dear," said the lady. "We've heard very little about you, actually. Jay is so seldom forthcoming about his friends. I'm sorry. I believe all I know is your name."

"It's no worry!" said Ellen with what she presumed to be a radiant and dignified smile. "I have always preferred to represent myself after all. I am an actress from Pennsylvania! My father is a mail carrier and my mother is a bombadier!"

Jay and his mother exchanged a glance, and then Jay turned to give Ellen a spirited rendition of the same surprised stare. The elder Mr. Harrey stood paunchy and tall above them, seeming to be locked in a perpetual frown; whether this was an accessory of business or indicative of a bad temper, Ellen did not know. She looked from Jay to his father, and saw a certain likeness, as if the father was a version of the son reprised after thirty years of staring at an ugly fence. She thought that this was how Jay would look in time if he were to become a Vice President. She thought the father was revolting. Ellen emitted a sparkling laugh, and noticed that they were standing next to a grand piano. She wondered when it had arrived.

"How strange you are an actress," Mrs. Harrey said, "because Mr. Harrey has just purchased controlling interest in a small production company. They are going to release a film in the summer. Isn't that strange?"

Ellen placed her hand on Mr. Harrey's arm, almost shivering with the decision to do it, "You know, Mr. Harrey, I have always had a theory about the marketing of films. Perhaps it can be of some use to you."

"What is that?" asked Mr. Harrey, without moving his upper lip.

"Well," said Ellen, glancing around at her little group, eyes ablaze with passion and charisma, "I have always found it so disingenuous how movie ads showcase positive reviews in such a lewd and suspicious manner. You know, 'a knock-your-socks-off-action-thrill-ride-of-a-lifetime' says Ann Peaslee of the *Whatnot Times*. That sort of thing."

"Yes," said Jay, apparently enthralled by her new life.

"Well," she said, speaking to Mr. Harrey senior, "I have always felt that a really smart film company would showcase their most negative reviews in the same way, at once indicting the insincerity of the other ads, and asserting an ironic disposition for the film, and definitely raising the interest level, don't you think?"

"Give an example," intoned Mr. Harrey.

"Alright," said Ellen, repressing more sparkling laughter with an obvious finger to the lips, "suppose you ran an ad that said 'Horrible beyond words' says the *L.A. Times*. 'Worse than being boiled alive' says the *Boston Globe*."

Ellen looked down, and then lifted her eyelashes to Mr. Harrey, "It is just a silly idea I know, just my silly notion of what could light the public on fire, but perhaps it is revolutionary. Perhaps it is just what you have been looking for?"

Mr. Harrey nodded, and then placed his arm around his wife, and then laughed. He laughed, and nodded, and let his eyes soften to Ellen. "Oh, I see," he said. "Yes, yes, very entertaining!"

"Jay," said Ellen, moving quickly to introduce new energy to the room, "Introduce me to some of your friends, won't you? I'm so anxious to welcome everyone to our new home. It's so nice to meet you, Mr. and Mrs. Harrey. So lovely to meet you."

Jay introduced Ellen to his friends. Ellen immediately identified them as computer nerds. Ellen widened her eyes, and attempted to telegraph the words *Girls like me would have sex with guys like you.*

She said, "Yes, Tim, I have often felt that if the Devil had a real business mind, he would option condominium space on the banks of the River Styx. Can you imagine the market value? The postmodern vacation spot. Tahiti? Absolutely not. It's the City of Dis this season, my dear. Ha ha!"

She said, "Yes Rob, I majored in Physics."

She said, "A commercial site is a criminal waste of bandwidth without active content. I absolutely agree."

She was calling on all her reserves. She was applying a fire to her internal organs, so that the steam escaped from her mouth. She floated from group to group throughout the downstairs of the house. She named people funny nicknames, touched people's wrists, truly truly met them with her eyes, and fluttered gaily on the point of laughter at every point of conversation. The true audience here, she thought, is composed of Jay and Molly. They have not kidnapped a tarnished bit of metal. No, it is a radiant jewel they have captured. And only now they see it. They see it!

After the party, Molly left quickly. All the guests were polite, happy, satiated. Ellen had never felt so ecstatic in her life almost. She could not remember another time when she had been an unqualified success, when she had felt so utterly completely unconnected. She sat, by the door, after bowing her head slightly and meeting the gaze of the final guest to leave. She used the toe of one shoe to push off the heel strap of the other, and then removed the second shoe with her hand. With both shoes dangling from her wrist, she met Jay's troubled gaze as he came into the foyer.

He said, "Did you have a good time?"

She said, "Yes."

He said, "Why did you leave the party?"

She said, "I was trying to escape."

"But you just couldn't manage it," he said. He didn't ask it, he said it.

"No."

"It was too thrilling a party. You just couldn't miss it," he said.

"I—"

"You had to meet my parents. They're such nice people."

"I wanted—"

Jay stood there at his height, looking down at her rather deflated self, crumpled on the chair in the foyer, and he was so very handsome. She thought she saw behind the craziness some other thing, some awareness that made her want to be aware with him, to find that thing and own it and understand it. He wasn't really crazy, she thought.

"You don't have to be some...horrible butterfly," said Jay.

"What do you mean," she demanded, instantly aware of the fact that her makeup was smudged, her hair a fallen ruin, and her belly protruding slightly as she slouched on the chair. She sat up straight, so it was flat.

"I mean," he said, as obviously tired as he was irritated, "that you do not have to play at this. You can leave, and take yourself away from me, and return yourself to him. If I were an adroit kidnapper, and if you were a helpless victim, this would have all been otherwise. I would have expected you to stay, in those circumstances. I would have had bars, a chain, a gun, and ropes. A party? Please to god. It smacks of the amateur. It echoes Mollyisms. Please tell me I haven't set you up to be this wretched—be this contrived thing, this animated corpse."

"I thought—your parents—"

"My parents really like you now," he said, as if he was blaming her, "although they were a bit perturbed at having been left out of the nonexistent loop. Our meeting, our courtship: they wanted to hear it all. They think you'll fit right in."

"I would have told them about all that."

"I'm sure you would have," he said, still standing, vanquished in the foyer.

He laughed, shook his head, and went to the stairs, where he put his head down on the banister, leaning over so she could see only his back. With a supreme act of will, and final resistance to his calling of her bluff, she made another decision.

"I want to sleep with you, in your bed," she said. "I know tonight is supposed to be our first night together. Let's be Lucy and Ricky, with one exception."

"No striped pajamas," he said in monotone.

She stood up and went over to him in her bare feet and put her hand on the small of his back. It was the first time she had touched him by choice. His back was warm, his shirt thin.

"Come on," she said, stepping on the first stair. "Let's go to bed."

It was her voice talking, and her body moving, that led him upstairs. He bought the act, if only for convenience's sake, and followed her.

"You know," she said, as she folded the covers down and pulled off her shirt, "I really did major in Physics."

Chapter Ten

Note: In Orkala, the double vowel is pronounced as the long sound of the vowel. So for example, while the word "Orkala" is pronounced "Or-Kah-Lah," the word "Akaal" is pronounced "Ah-kayl."

When Stef fell asleep, he was on the island of Orkala. It happened all the time. It was neither upsetting nor a mystery. When he fell asleep, he dreamed himself onto the island, near the coastal city of Azkau, across the Ounu Sea from the continent of Ylomi, in the world his people called Ubaan. Stef lived in Ubaan long before the rise of the Emperor Malcas, in a time when the mantics were still living in the four territories, before the world was harnessed, when one could still see Kurkou freely moving on the island, and travel to the other territories was incredibly difficult. Orkala, of course, was particularly isolated in those days, being an island, and being largely influenced by The Seven and their Muse. To travel on the water was forbidden, though ships from both Muu and Iros dropped anchor in inlets and bays around the South of the island on a regular basis, and sometimes one even saw a mariner from the southern lands of Adwee.

In Orkala, Stef had no knowledge of microwave ovens, BorgWarner transmissions, and Federal Express. He was mostly concerned with scimitars, footpaths, tame Bazkaats, and Raarzaazuta, his girlfriend. Asleep, he remembered everything about Orkala, from military history to eating utensils. Awake, he remembered a lot of it, but not all of it. For this reason, he enjoyed going to sleep. Life was like a difficult puzzle whose simple solution was masked by layers of irrelevant ceremony. If in the end, if all he must do is kill a dragon and rescue a princess, then why did his path inevitably wind through twisting passageways and rooms full of spikes which could only be retracted by solving the Puzzle of the Bullfrog? Why were there never stairs? If in the end, if all he must do is get money, fall in love, make children, build a house, and then die, then why must he understand a fax machine, collect beer cans, learn algebra? In Orkala, the rhythms were simpler. In Orkala, there were no ink pens and paper forms, no cash registers and combination locks, no internet and electronic banking. Places and people could be accessed directly, by speech and foot travel, and people who were betrothed were eventually married.

He went to sleep and dreamed about Orkala, on the shore. He lay on his back on a flat mat which covered the sand beneath him, and when he opened his eyes he stared into the sky, a bright afternoon. Beside him lay Raarzaazuta on a mat of her own. His thick hand rested on her tiny one. She had woven the mats out of a sharp-smelling weed which kept the bugs away, but in the hot, still silence of the day there were no insects about, and the smell of the mats seeped into the air, turning it sweet and thick. Behind his head, the tree line rustled and hushed as the coastal wind ebbed and flowed, and the waves broke smoothly, only ripples down beyond his feet. It was so tranquil that Raarzaazuta must have been asleep. And she was. Turning his head to the side, he saw her pale eyelids tremble in sleep, and her rosy mouth twitch as she pursued some dreaming argument. She had not taken off her small breastplate and her leather greaves, even for an afternoon at the sea. In this fierce attire, and fast asleep, she looked to him like an armored doll, blonde hair falling off the mat onto the sand, heavy boots pulling one foot from the other to rest askew.

He pulled his hand away from her and sat up, glancing up and down the beach to get his bearings. He saw their picnic bucket several feet behind them, and their Bazkaats drowsing in the shade where they were tied. Beyond the tree line, the forest stretched on for a piece in shiny leaves and giant stalks of the occasional Ulo tree, and then became a valley between two hills which pointed out east to sea as headlands. He recognized this spot clearly—a quick morning's ride from the tower of the fireman, her brother, at the top of the valley. Raarzaazuta and Stef had often visited here in the two years he had been courting her. There was a stream just forty yards into the trees which wound around and joined a larger one, emptying into the sea just south of here. He remembered so clearly arriving, through the thick emerald foliage that seemed to get more impossibly dense as they neared the sea, only to stop abruptly as the earth turned to sand and the brightness of the beach burst upon them. They must have come out in the morning, had a swim, eaten lunch, and then fallen asleep in the sun. He let himself drop back down on his side, sighing with absolute contentment, resting his head on his elbow to look at her. This close to her, he could not help reaching out a hand to touch her, trace the bones of her little face with his rough thumb, an imposition she would never have allowed when conscious. To his surprise, her eyes opened slightly, but she didn't jerk away or smack his hand, just looked at him sleepily between her eyelashes, and sighed, a little smile playing across her lips. As he was watching her, letting his hand stay close, a shadow followed the smile, and in an instant she was sitting up, standing, brushing herself off and folding the mat in haste.

"Tuz, Tuz, Tuz!" she cried. "How can I have fallen asleep! It is so late! What will Akaal say!"

Stef stood, grudgingly, and frowned at her, "Akaal? What about him?"

She glared at him and tightened up her mouth, her whole body going stiff and militant as she smacked at her legs and boots to clean them, "You know. It's his meditation. Probably past by now."

Stef nodded with mock solemnity, then winked at her and reached out an arm to grab her and pull her toward him, saying, "Oh, right. Meditation. Can't miss meditation." He attempted a winning smile and grasped her wrist, but she shrank away from him in irritation and stuffed her mat into the bucket, pulling her boots laboriously out of the sand with each step. Looking at his mat, and him standing there disappointed, she frowned.

"I have to go on ahead," she said. "I'm late. Can you bring all this stuff, and just clean up here, and then come on back? Thanks."

Waving her arm vaguely at the bucket and the beach, she turned on her heel, and struggled over the sand briskly. She grabbed the rope and untied her Bazkaat, threw her leg around his back, and the beast stood up from its crouch, blowing quietly through his nostrils and stamping one leg. Gripping its body with her legs, one hand around its neck for balance, she turned it toward the valley, dug in her heels, plunged into the forest, and disappeared. Stef stayed on the beach.

He picked up the picnic bucket and sat back down on his mat, crossing his legs and holding it in his lap. Pulling her mat back out of the bucket, he flopped it open and threw it on the sand next to him. If she had stayed asleep, it might have been too late to go back to the tower when she woke up. They could have built a fire by the sea, roasted fruits from the forest, spent the night on the sand. But this had never happened before. Usually, she kept her eye on the sun, and bustled him into action in time to reach the tower with an hour to spare.

Her devotion to her brother was a constant specter. Stef did not suspect her of sleeping with him, but she would not sleep away from him either. She wouldn't even talk about marriage, would rather leave him hanging than leave the tower. She was the fireman's sister, a nobleman's daughter, and he was a common swordsman, personal guard to the Templar in Azkau. He couldn't make demands on her. In English, Raarzaazuta meant "Tomorrow River." He called her Zuta.

Stef wondered what would happen if he was sitting in The Joyride on his stool by the door, on a sullen night in Toledo, and there was a noise outside of a thousand people, soldiers and citizens, women, and even children waving little toy light sabers, all chanting, "Kill Stef!" at the top of their lungs. He would keep the door closed, and peek out through the window, and see the throng of bodies pulsing and crushed together, animated by their collective hollering. They would push up against the building, threatening to break in the windows, knock down the door. They would spy him at the window, reach in with long arms through broken glass, and drag him out into the street where they would kill him with guns, clubs, spears, sticks, and lances. The women would throw ceramic vases onto his head, and the children would stamp on his fingers. Stef sat with his back to the wall, the door to his right and the window on his left, and listened all night.

In the fireman's tower, Zuta and Akaal behaved as if Stef wasn't even there. The three sat in a large room after supper, drinking thick Ulo sap from dark pewter goblets. Stef's chair was low and lush and close to the fire, but the brother and sister reclined together on a long sofa in the shadows, his head in her lap, her eyes almost glowing in the dim light, her fingers in his hair. She had removed her armor after supper and was now wrapped in a red robe, her hair falling loosely around her face. When the fire died down, Akaal muttered the word, "Uttaabaarznaro," and it sprang back to life, momentarily scorching Stef's protruding legs with its heat. There was no wood in the fireplace, no fuel and no smoke. It was all Akaal's doing. Behind them, the room was cold. The walls were dark, and the rug stretched over flagstones chilling to touch. In the center of the tower, this room may have held one hundred people laughing and talking, if all the torches around the walls were lit. Akaal could have lit them with a word, but he didn't, as if he wanted it dark, as if he wanted them to be somber.

"I don't think it's ever been done before," Akaal was saying, his eyes closed and his body slack. "You can't just give up your abilities—the training, the information, it's all still there."

Zuta's eyes were fixed on the flame, and she said firmly, "You can do whatever you want to do. It's your choice. You choose to do it. You can choose not to do it."

Stef had heard this conversation before. Akaal wanted lately to give up being a fireman, unlearn his magic, drown the talismans of Kol, Uzu, and the other Seven, and be a normal person, swim in the ocean like they did, drink water, the rest of it. Zuta always told him just to do it, but she, apparently, didn't understand how difficult it was.

"It's not so easy," said Akaal with irritatingly affectionate patience. "I don't know how it will work. I am afraid to approach the Muse about it, and I am afraid to approach the gods."

"Just fade away," said Zuta, "Become a nobleman. Stay here in the tower, but have parties, burn wood, forget the spell words, take a wife."

Zuta stopped abruptly and Stef leaned forward to turn and look at her. Her face had brightened and she nodded, as if suddenly entranced by an idea.

"That's it! Take a wife!" she said, nudging Akaal off her lap and making him sit up. "Of course that's what you must do. Why didn't we think of this before? If you marry, you can't be a fireman anymore. It's against the law! It solves everything!"

Akaal rolled his eyes and sagged back against the sofa, stretching his legs. "Impossible," he said morosely. "Can you think of one single girl who would consider my courtship? Ridiculous."

Zuta stamped her bare foot on the floor, her face disgusted. Stef turned back to the fire and sank into his chair, holding his goblet in both hands on his chest.

"You are such a coward," she said, almost laughing but angry. "Won't you even try? I'm sure there's someone over there in that miserable stupid city who'd like to live here. I could ask around, maybe set you up with one of the dancers—"

Akaal stopped her, "The dancers know me as a fireman. What am I supposed to do, bring flowers to the next Nanonzo, and get one into a corner?" He lowered his voice and mocked, "Hello, I know you see me as the creepy and mysterious man who wears a robe of live embers, and I'm about to paint flames onto your naked breasts before you dance yourself into a religious hysteria, but would you like to accompany me to the tavern later?"

Zuta laughed.

"And anyway," Akaal continued, "It has to be instantaneous. I can't do fire if I am married, but I can't court if I do fire."

They both stayed silent for a moment, and Stef poked his head around the side of his chair to say, "I thought those rituals were supposed to be better than sex, anyway. What do you want a woman for?"

Akaal responded with a sneer and no words, but Zuta was not to be distracted.

"Well then," she said, slowly pointing with her finger, "What if Stef just goes and finds you a wife? Instantaneous...no courtship...perfect! He can nab one of those city girls, bring her out here, we'll make her see just how lucky she is, and you can marry her immediately. Next thing you know the Muse'll be knocking on your door, demanding your talismans, and you'll be free."

She bounced a bit on the sofa, squeezing her legs together and clapping with her little hands, "You can be a nobleman! No more magic. No more hinky spells. Real wood in the fireplace, and real water in the cellar. I love it."

Akaal was quiet. He may have been shaking his head, or he may have been nodding. Stef didn't know. He did know that if Akaal married, then Zuta would be his. With his job in Azkau, he could afford to buy a very respectable cottage, in town or in the hills, even build one right in this valley so she could be near Akaal. He didn't mind the daily ride into town—he was doing it now anyway just to see her, and riding back at night to his rooms over the Templar's offices, where the bachelor guards all lived. He even knew the girl he would choose—the Templar's mistress, Aano.

Stef didn't enjoy driving cars. He disliked the rigidity of four gears, the awkwardness of turning in a full circle just to leave a cul de sac, the fumes of the exhaust, and the windshield. He didn't like people swearing at him in traffic jams, and he didn't like the roads themselves—concrete, hot, and final. He preferred the sweaty and invigorating travel on a Bazkaat, through the lush valleys and dark mountains of Orkala. The Bazkaat had one speed, which was as fast as possible, and it was handy—it could spin full circle on the spot, using its tail for balance and support. The creature was built for climbing, and when on level ground its front legs dangled, like a kangaroo. On a steep grade the Bazkaat dug in with all fours, lunging and dragging, and on the valley floor it ran in a side-to-side lurch, pulsing off its powerful back legs. Riding a Bazkaat was more like clutching onto it, with legs and arms, feet hooked over its stifle joints like stirrups. The tame ones were affectionate, and could be lead on ropes. Sometimes Stef imagined himself hurtling down South Main in Toledo on his Orkalan mount, zooming past The Joyride with a clank of his scimitar and a thud of the beast's foot on concrete. He would leave behind the scent of the island forest.

With a dark mask over his eyes, Stef lurked outside the tavern in Azkau. Fires blazed in barrels down the street, people wandered around on foot and some lead Bazkaats. They drank sap from cups, ate roasted pork straight from the bones, and chattered happily at each other. Rude music came from some of the buildings, and others bulged with people making merry inside.

The light from a fire outside the tavern made deep shadows in which Stef could hide, and he finally saw the Templar approaching with his entourage. He was a stern man, stiff with political authority, gaunt with anxiety, and tall. With him Stef saw Aano, a slender, petulant girl making her way through the crowded street and grasping the Templar's arm. The tavern was for men only, and he left her at the door when he went in, to find her own entertainment in the street. Stef watched her sigh, and as the other girls wandered off to dance or dally, he watched her stay, lingering outside the building, standing near the fire. She always did this, hanging around chatting with the Templar's bodyguards, and sometimes spending long periods of time apparently lost in thought. It was how Stef had come to know her. She had often talked to him about life outside this city, in the next valley over or the next, or even up in the mountains. He was favored among the Templar's guards, and was not refused conversation, even with the Templar himself. He felt respect for this man, who was deep in his work and yet beset with romantic difficulties, as he failed to settle down with one consort or another.

He saw her step up to the fire, and make weird gestures in front of it with her hands. He wondered, not for the first time, what she was thinking about when she went off like that. He had always admired her fondly, despite her oddities and her off-putting airs, because she was so confused. While she loved the Templar, he thought, she didn't seem happy in the city. He thought that when he took her to the tower, there might be a rescue and there might not. If there was a rescue, then the Templar would pay attention to her, would decide on her among the others, and maybe that would make them happy. If there was no rescue, then the girl would be with Akaal, and would know what life was like outside the city. Either way, it was good for her. And if she took Akaal away from Zuta, it was good for him too.

She finally left the fire and with a last glance at the tavern door wandered away from the building. He moved toward her slowly, and when she had joined a clump of people walking, he took her by the wrist, clamped a hand over her mouth, and began to run toward the shadows at the end of the street. She came silently. She was heavier than he had imagined, but he dragged her with him through the city, past the main square in alleys, and down to the beachhead where his Bazkaat was waiting. Then he released her.

"What are you doing?" she said, gasping for air. "I am the Templar's consort! Who are you?"

He touched his mask and didn't speak. Instead he quickly bound her hands together with some rope, and then jerking her around behind him, he pulled her arms over his head, so that he was within their circle, and they rested around his arms below the shoulder.

"What are you doing?" she said again. "Please, don't hurt me!"

Without a word, he straddled the Bazkaat which lurched onto its feet under the weight of their two bodies, and set off at a mad pace down the beach. It would take longer to reach the tower by this route, but it would be safer. The Orkalans didn't visit the water at night, and most stayed away even in the sunlight. Thudding down the sandy stretch, he clutched his mount around its neck and dug his knees into its side, struggling to keep both of them anchored. The girl behind him gripped him tightly with her arms until he almost couldn't breathe, but she stayed on, and he felt wildly triumphant. There was no struggle, and no need to hurt her or scare her. After several miles of solid speed he turned the Bazkaat and it ducked into the trees.

Stef liked to watch a smoker who was having trouble lighting her cigarette. He liked watching her bend away from the wind, struggle with fingernails and childproof lighters, hunch over her cigarette, try to get under her collar, all of it. The most interesting thing to observe was the look that smokers get on their faces just after they have successfully lit up and just as they are breathing in on the first drag. They always look around. They scan the horizon. In this act of looking,

Stef is reminded of the Biblical story of the river drinkers. A group of thirsty warriors were sent down to the riverside to quench their thirst. The ones who leaned down and lapped like dogs at the water were ejected from the group. The ones who cupped water in their hands, and lifted it to their faces so they could drink while still watching for enemies, were promoted. Why do people look across rivers? Why do they look out to sea? There's no reason for it anymore. All enemies are known, and none of them pose a threat to any horizon visible from Toledo, Ohio. But the smokers keep an eye out anyway.

Stef slept and dreamed he stood outside the tower, in the small clearing in front of its tall iron entrance. All around, the trees loomed in, but just in front of the tower the trees had been chopped down long ago, so that one could see down over the hill, over the valley, to the sea. Aano had been released from a short captivity in the wine cellar, and was at that moment hanging Akaal's ceremonial robes out in the sunlight to "breathe." She wasn't frightened by the gloom of the building, or turned off by the looming statues and symbols inside. Stef could see that she had been opening windows, sweeping out passageways, bringing fresh flowers into the sanctuary. Maybe she liked being lady of the manor, or maybe she didn't want to make trouble for herself. Stef didn't know.

As he stood watching, the heavy front door creaked open and Zuta came rushing out, her bright hair glinting in the sun, to jump into his arms. As he held her tightly and lifted her off the ground in his embrace, she whispered in his ear, "It's happened! The Muse has been here, and he took away everything—Akaal's talismans—everything! He can't even walk into a temple!"

"What?" he asked, setting her down. She looked excited, happy, delirious.

"We sent away all the servants, and..." she drifted off, glancing over at the other girl, who was finished with the robes and walking over to join them, "Aano is here, and she likes it here...she's doing just fine."

Stef saw Zuta clench her teeth a bit and force a smile. Aano approached them and waved nervously in his direction.

"I know that you are my kidnapper," she said, smiling at him brightly. "It was a very wrong thing to do, and has ruined my life in horribly unforgivable ways."

"Um, yes yes," Zuta interrupted, wincing as if the listening to the girl was painful. "Ah, Aano, I believe Akaal needs warm water for his bath. Perhaps you could attend to it?"

Aano gave Zuta a withering look, winked at Stef, and disappeared inside the tower, leaving them alone.

"This is great," said Stef, holding up a bag of fruit. "I brought grapes, and there are races today in town. If we leave now, we can make it in time for the betting. And you don't have to be back before dark—we could make a night of it, maybe visit my cousin for supper—"

"Are you crazy?" she cut him off, glancing at the door which closed quietly behind Aano. "I'm not leaving him here with her! She's a complete nutcase. What kind of person gets kidnapped and likes it? She's no good for Akaal, and she likes him way too much. She actually thinks the marriage meant something, and she's planning on staying forever. No, I can't leave. At any moment, she might try to seduce him, and if she...just come inside. We can eat grapes anywhere— we don't have to go to town to eat grapes."

She started to pull him by the hand toward the door but he wouldn't go. The day stretched into days and into weeks. Aano seemed to enjoy the tower for a while, but she grew restless and became silent again as nothing changed. She took to staring into flames, and whispering things to herself. At times, she argued with Akaal, who was experiencing problems of his own. Though he was no longer officially a fireman, he still retained some lingering power. If he concentrated too hard on one particular thing, he singed it, even Stef's bracers which he was attempting to repair. If he sat too long in the bath it grew hot, and began to bubble. The people in town still revered him as holy, or now shunned him as cursed, so that his visits to town were a sham of the noble reception they had all imagined. Once, on his way through the forest, Stef came upon Akaal alone in a clearing, frantically feeding a giant bonfire with chunks of wood and sod. He was calling out, in dark foreign words, to the gods, Stef thought. He didn't stay to see if Akaal received an answer. In all of this dissatisfaction Zuta stayed intent on keeping Aano out of Akaal's bed, keeping Akaal away from open flames, and keeping Stef perpetually at a distance. It wore on him, the disappointment.

If he had to defend Toledo, he would defend it with walls against the lake. Any enemy would be met outside the eastern gates, with malice. He would be a knight of Lord Toledo, protecting his honor from the adjacent realms of Cleveland and Columbus. He would bear the colors of his Lord. Amidst the mass of warriors and the many standards hovering overhead, the Duke of Northwood, the Earl of Buck Road, a great banner would fly, around which a great multitude of great, mailed men would gather: the yellow flame-wreathed skull of Toledo. There Stef the banner bearer, a massive soldier clad in black and bearing a horned helm upon his shoulders, would stand, a black iron hammer gripped in his opposing hand. With a piercing shout through visor-concealed lips, Stef would urge the color guard of Toledo onwards, down the plains to meet the loathsome men of Cleveland, come to take their lakeside fortress.

Eager to wreak their violence upon the enemy, Stef and the soldiers of his color guard would advance rapidly towards the oncoming soldiers, their scimitars and axes vigorously shaken overhead. With the banner's thick haft in his mailed grip, the black-horned Stef would throw his bulk forward, hurrying in his rush to intercept the Lord Cleveland, and the squad of guards around him.

Furious screams and valorous grunts would explode from the mouths of the Toledo color guard as their ranks crashed violently into those of Cleveland's men. The ringing of steel upon helm and shield would become nearly overwhelming, the confusion of swift, blurred movements, jostling, shoving, and shouted orders and insults from every direction nearly enough to numb the senses. With precise speed and calculated accuracy, Stef the standard bearer would lunge through the tangling bodies and directly for the Lord Cleveland, the spiked head of his heavy hammer thrust towards the man's midsection.

In real life, battles didn't happen this way. But if they did, that is how Stef would fight them.

In Orkala, Stef traveled on foot from Azkau to the tower, in the company of city guards, and the Captain of the Guard was a pert little woman named Onol. They brushed stiffly along the forest trail, the guards marching in sloppy formation and the Captain lingering at the rear to talk to Stef. It had been years since Stef had made this trip on foot.

"If they aren't armed, we will leave the guards outside," she said, one arm folded across her torso as she walked, the other hand on her chin. "I think that if the fireman is actually powerless, then you and I could take the girl alone."

"I'd rather have them in there," said Stef with a frown. "You never know. He could have friends of which we know nothing."

"Perhaps," she said, peering at him sideways, "Are you sure he will be alone, with the girl?"

"Yes," he told her. "He will be alone." Raarzaazuta was in town, looking for Stef, probably.

"Your information is valuable," mused the Captain of the Guard. "I will remember this to the Templar. You may very well receive a promotion, or maybe be invited to join his personal guard. He seems so intent on getting this girl back—no other consort will please him these days."

Stef thought he would remember it to the Templar himself, but didn't say anything. If she had forgotten who his employer was, it was no matter. This woman struck him as insufferably enchanted with herself, and her hints about "remembering him to the Templar" reminded Stef of how cozily she and the Templar had shared the search for Aano, how close she had come to hooking him for herself.

When they reached the tower, there was a compromise. Four of the guards remained outside, and four approached the door with Stef and Onol, where she pounded on it fiercely.

"Open all inside," she barked. "Deliver your prisoner or we shall take her by force."

There was a silence in the tower, and in the forest as well, broken only by the cawing of a distant bird, and the ragged sound of faraway surf. Onol rapped again on the stone door, using the heel of her hand and producing a deep thudding noise.

"Open all inside," she repeated. "Or we shall come in with swords drawn!"

The door shifted a bit, creaked, and was dragged in by an unseen hand. The hall of the tower opened up before them, dim compared to the light of day, but no longer as somber as Stef could remember it. There was a bright woven mat behind the doorway, and someone had been scuffing their feet on it. Stef and Onol peered into the opening, the guards behind them moving up a bit. As they drew closer, and stepped over the threshold, the head of Aano appeared from behind the door, and she said, "Hello."

Her hair was brushed down straight and tame, and she wore a white robe tied around with a gold rope. At the sight of her, Onol leaped into action. She grabbed the girl by the rope around her waist, jerked her out into the daylight, and tossed her to one of the guards, simultaneously kicking the tower door wide open and training her eyes around the room. Stef couldn't stop himself from looking at the girl, and as Onol shouted, "Keep her safe! Take her to the forest immediately!" he saw the girl smiling slightly as she stumbled off, so passive in her transfer from one's idea to another's, so lacking in hesitance or eagerness. He hoped in that moment that she would be happy with the Templar now that his attentions were acute. "Tuz!" yapped Onol in his direction, "Can you not come quicker than that?"

He stepped up to her side, and with one arm on his arm she advanced, quietly, slowly through the entranceway, and then into the main hall, where the torches were all ablaze, and the scent of fresh fruit pervaded the air. A silly banquet spread lay on the broad huge table. Someone had been making fun with the old cutlery and plates, using noble tools to eat grapes and pomegranates, and daisies were scattered here and there. The Captain searched the scene slowly, tensing her face as she glared behind doors and furniture for her prey. But he came down the stairs, half dressed in a tunic and mismatched socks, his hair rumpled. He grumbled something, peering at the Captain and at Stef, and shook his head impatiently. Stef acted immediately, before the guards behind him could react.

"A spell!" he shouted. "The fireman speaks a spell!"

A long spear, launched from behind Stef's ear, sped true and swift across the room, and before Akaal could reach the bottom step his body was skewered on it, and fell the remaining distance to the floor.

As Stef and the Captain rushed toward the man, he said, "She wants..." and then his eyes closed and his head lolled. The Captain knelt quickly at his head, grabbing his throat in her hand, intent on listening. His heart still beat a few moments more, but he was quickly dead. She looked up at Stef and said, "Well spotted. The Templar will be pleased."

Akaal was buried in a ceremonial spot, but fire never flickered on his grave, as it did with other firemen who died as righteous men. Stef quit his job as the Templar's guard, and moved into the tower with Raarzaazuta, where they lived out their days in wealth and wedded peace. Zuta realized soon after Akaal's death that a life with Stef was all she had ever wanted. She gave up her hostile warlike attire, and bore a child, who learned to swim at an early age, and became a great knight. The Templar wedded Aano, deserting all his other women, and they lived their life out in Azkau, where Aano became known as an adventuress and a cartographer, committing much unknown territory to the city's library records, and having many exciting adventures.

Chapter Eleven

Ellen lay naked on the bed like a wild thing being absolutely still. Instead of limp, she was taut. Instead of acquiescent, she was tousled. The deep deep secret under every secret fact was that she had never had sex with anyone but Martin. Not even Martin knew. In a supreme effort of will, and conjuring all the strength she'd absorbed from her experience of being the life of the party for the first time ever, she kicked the covers down to the bottom of the bed and threw her hands up toward the headboard, exposed. She was nervous to the point of explosion.

In order to be a true kidnapped person she would have to have sex with a sort of mad abandon that implied all kinds of things about possession (how it wasn't really possible, even though she was kidnapped), and choice (how she was making it, even though she was kidnapped), and exploration (how it was all she was really interested in, even now, as she was in the process of being kidnapped). She would have to convince Jay, through various sexual practices, that it was really nothing to her being out like this away from Martin. That she had had many partners, too numerous to discuss, and that sex for her was not a frantic mixture of desire and panic, but a well-considered process that through repetition and practice had become rote and therefore transcendent. Like riding a horse, where you go for years thinking about each separate act and action, and then at last it becomes automatic and you can really ride.

She flicked her head back and forth a bit and moaned in practice. She lay still. Then she flung herself up into a sitting position and let her hair fall unsorted around her face. She climbed up so that she was kneeling and the naked expanse of her torso felt chilly and exciting. The hair around her shoulders touched her and tickled her in a strange room in a strange house for the first time. She jounced on the bed a little to check its sproinginess. Too much sproing and the sex became silly, she knew. But it was firm. She imagined them both in a motel room in St. Louis, one of those long motels where you park in front of your room and walk in, and there is fake wood paneling and a bathroom at the back. She would be bored, perpetually rolling her eyes and sitting with her long legs spread apart and her elbows on her knees and smoking. He would go into the bathroom and be there for a long time staring at himself in the mirror and doubting himself as a person. Then he would come out in a tight ribbed tank top and jeans, and she could imagine him clearly like this because he had one of those male model bodies—loose and gaunt. He would launch some quip at her and she would quip back in a way that would make them both chuckle in spite of themselves, something about the raw red carpet hiding blood stains, or about the big print on the wall showing someone's ugly kitchen. After taking a long time to stub out her cigarette she would fall back across the bed, and he would come over and put his hands over her arms and lie up against her for the very first time.

Of course, in order to be a true kidnapped person, this grittiness would eventually be dispelled by a poignant moment of afterglow, or a state of mutual danger, or some kind of dialogue between them in a car, later. But it didn't happen now—now was the sex which was mechanical and dirty and aggressive and profane. This was what was expected of her, after all. She was a hostage in a terrible situation, with pressures and dangers all around. If she didn't agree to his sexual advances, she would surely be killed. Maintaining this thought, she wouldn't have to fade into dewy moments until their second or third tryst. She made her eyes slitty and small and looked at the bathroom door with shuddering apathy. She wanted to be sitting when he came out against the head of the bed with her legs crossed and absolutely naked. In the kind of pose that makes pubic hair look so belligerent and abased. She raised herself up on her knees and her hands to crawl up there so that when Jay came out of the bathroom in a blue terrycloth robe, she was peeking at him backwards through her legs.

Jay, of course, had only been sleeping with prostitutes. And he had been standing, staring at himself in the bathroom mirror, in his terrycloth robe, assaulting himself with accusations and horrible threats. If the girl had been acting strangely at the party, then she was messing it all up, and if it was unnatural for her then why the charade, why the ignominious pretensions? But perhaps, perhaps, perhaps it was all charade anyway, the smiles, the hope, the big open eyes and all the doorbell ringing and vegetable dipping, and the kind of lights in the house that dispel the monitor glare, so to pretend, for her, was a natural act, caused by a magnetic force from the strength of the furniture, the house, the subdivision, and the world. For, he thought, who am I to make assumptions about these clothes? I have only recently bought them myself. I should be good! Set an example! She's not the one who started this!

He took a razor from the bathroom mirror cabinet where he had placed it before when he was arranging things. It was a brand new razor, black and sharp. He set the razor down on the bathroom sink and picked up the can of shaving gel, squirting out some green gel into his left palm. If only the girl would behave properly, and if only the proper behavior was genuine enough to fool him, so he could think of her as a real girl, but also think of her as fitting into his kitchen. He smeared the gel over his face and stared himself down in the mirror, willing her to behave. If the girl would behave, he could come into the room and switch out the light, slide under the covers which were tidy and blue, and stretch his feet down into the bottom of the bed. He could stretch, sigh, roll across, and his hand would fall onto her shoulder where she was sleeping. She would surprise him by being awake and they would wrap up together in what Jay knew was a hug, which was warm and nice and belonging, and involving different parts of the body. Then with her warm and invisible beside him he would kiss her with lips only, penis poking out gently from in the cotton pajamas, and there would be a fold of her nightgown that was really an opening, and his penis would go in there, and in one soft push they would be finished with it and locked together for more hugging, and under that blue comforter, there would be quiet.

It thrilled him remotely to think about that moment, when it was all over, when he and his fiancée, in their house which was dark, rested next to each other, with copulation past and all behaviors finished, wrapped up tight in the matching linens, and in the wall clock and the silent air, deep in the suburbs, hidden in multitudes of others just like them, all in the quiet night, with swollen feet from a long day, and hearts so good and warm. He could imagine, in the bright cold bathroom, what this would be like. If only she would behave, then she would not call out his name or anything, or feel entirely passionate, or thrash about. A man who sleeps with prostitutes exclusively is accustomed to getting what he wants. Jay rinsed off his hand and began to shave, scraping away all the unkind thoughts and traditional skepticism, trying to forget what she had been like and only remember what she could be like, always forever, if only she would keep herself calm, and not be frantic, and not annoy him or be stupid. He emerged from the bathroom clean and smelling fresh, like a good husband, and turned out the light.

Stef and Zuta reclined in a glittering cave on the island of Orkala, far back from the coast and across the ridge from Akaal's bleak tower. The carcass of a giant bear steamed beside them and they drank hot sap from their travelling cups. They would never go back to the tower or to Azkau. They would live forever in the unmapped mountains killing bears and washing in streams. Stef pulled a wad of cloth away from a large gash on his shoulder and winced, but gritted his teeth and ate the pain. Zuta purred and took the cloth away from him, dipping it in an herbal mixture she had prepared over the fire and handing it back. The smell of the herbs sent strong currents through Stef's thick body, as this was their mating ritual, and they would mate on the floor of the cave as soon as the bleeding stopped. He sighed and relaxed against the bear's warm back, fiddling with his scimitar peacefully and sticking the cloth back against his wound. "Zuta," he said, "Dance for me."

WELCOME NANO-PERVS AND GLAMATRONS!
To Solid Steel Saturday at the Den of Desiccated Debauchery! Brought to you live via hologram from the Prince of Knives' Sin Salon, we bring you our star cyborg sex-pot! You know her as the girl warrior, you've seen her as the jungle princess, you loved her as the maiden-stealing maniac, now deliver yourself, ladies and gentlemen, to the flirtations, the gyrations, the explications of The Mechanical Mistress, Molly Harrey! May I remind you, denizens, as our transmission stabilizes, and as the music begins to grind your groin and gel your generosity, to tip your waitresses but don't tip the dancer. She's not really there!

Stef drank deeply and watched her move through the cave, humming quietly under her breath. Her body, encased in its leather armor and fur cloak, jerked and twitched in the forms of a long-forgotten ritual dance, or one she was only now inventing. He grunted in approval as she shed the cape, letting it fall from her fingers onto the floor of the cave where it draped, waiting for them. The air in the cave was still, and every tap of her foot on the rock floor echoed with her murmured tune, forming a rhythm. He pushed himself back against the bear, peeling the cloth away from his wound which seemed now staunched. Setting his cup aside, he joined her by stamping his foot with her dancing beat, and making clicking noises in his throat. He pulled off his breastplate, easing it over the wound, and began to work on his shirt.

The lights shimmer, and suddenly, she is there! All eyes grip the girl made of vinyl and steel! Who can flip herself up onto the stage she has made out of her apartment and a porno pole! Without even grunting! Though she is metal! Though she is amazing! She is still alive! She struts down the catwalk! With too many joints and muscles! To be real! Does a handstand! But both legs come down on the wrong side! Revealing every inch of crack laid out in vinyl so shiny and hot! Can she right herself! Yes! Only a cyborg! Can achieve it! Her boots! Thigh-high! Her dress! Tiny! Everything is clicking! It is all so very smooth!

Zuta was now beckoning him gently, playing with the folds of her costume and deliberately circling nearer to the robe on the floor. Her hums had now evolved into a high whine, and she grinned coyly as she turned away to unfasten her jerkin. When she slipped it off he could see the bones in her back and the way they were small and cold and he crept over to the cloak and lay down on it so that she was circling around him. Looking up at her reverently he held out a hand but she continued to turn and whirl, now keening. She unbuckled her belt and her pants fell to her ankles. She kicked them off, a nervous laugh breaking up her song. At last she approached him, naked and dropping to her knees on the cloak before him, and he took her down.

She growls! She whirrs! She bares her teeth! There are lots! But it is the pole that she attacks! Climbs it up and up! Until she is so high! Only the mirror! Can reflect her back! And no one in the audience can even see her! Except her mechanic! Of course! Up there she winds her legs around the pole! With incredible flair! And a hard grip! And swings free and out! Down! Down! Falling! Crucified! Ten thousand images in holograph! Not a single one of them real! She hangs from one leg! From one arm! Amazing! The music thunders! The cyborg slides! And makes long tongues at him! He cannot help! But reach out! And touches! Only a shimmer!

Jane lay on the bed flat, with Martin's fist around her throat, his penis in her vagina, and his other hand rammed into her anus. Even though she had recently had a cold, even though she had never had three fingers in her ass before, only one, she lay quiet and still and managed not to choke. Every part of her, from her good little butt to her decently closed eyes, aspired to help Martin recreate every brutal act of rape he had ever committed against Ellen in all the years they had been together. This is how Ellen must have felt, thought Jane, this is exactly how Ellen must have experienced it when he was doing it to her, and her legs like mine fifteen degrees separated, and never more, and never fully closed. In his stark, spartan room in the center of this jet black apartment building, and covered with little drops of his demonic sweat, Jane assumed a beatific air of calm. Her limbs went stiffly into place, exactly rotating at the shoulder and the hip, but never breaking at the elbow, only bending slightly at the knee. Her head she turned back and forth, but never nodded.

In her victim head, Jane knew that raping was terrible and raping was long, and that any long terrible raping was likely to prompt a girl to take off without warning, ditch a car on a freeway shoulder, and fly into the night. If it had been Jane, if it had been Jane lying there all those dismal years, experiencing one misery after another, then Jane would not have run away. She would have persevered, bravely, through every stiff night of woe, through every dark perversion, with her eyes still closed, a shining halo wrapped around her head. She would have cocked her wrist just so and left it flexed there, either by her side or up in the air, like a wave, forever lying flat.

Jane lay under Martin's snarling face, peeking out just enough to see the hatred, and she shifted her stiff limbs under him, never cracking the pose of her ankles and wrists so that she could lie still again. Only a good quiet girl with a carefully arched foot could experience true horrors. When he pulled his fingers out and used that arm to grab her legs and hold them up high over her head, finding this rotation to provide him closer access, and pulled his penis out to watch his semen go all over, Jane gulped and shivered. It was warm, though, as it spattered.

Beneath the rationalizing and all the careful placement of this idea, Martin had suspected that sex with Jane would feel entirely wrong. But it didn't, because of vectors. Martin's penis, when it was hard, was very

very hard and straight. So it went right in. And when he was fucking her, his flat chest dampened by a mist of sweat, she was just as tall as Ellen ever was, and was also similar in that she had a vagina which was a hole into which he could put his penis with his eyes shut. He had once heard a Chief Petty Officer say that every butt had a hole in it, or else it didn't work. At the time, it had struck him as an odd thing to say, and pointless. Now, he was glad that Jane had a hole in her, and that she worked, and that this was guaranteed by her being female, just like buttholes were guaranteed by the nature of butts. To Martin, this was not a crude comparison, because everything having to do with bodies was necessarily crude, so neither side of the analogy suffered.

In Martin's bedroom, the wood was dark but the lights were bright. Jane lay naked on the bed with her legs hanging over the edge, spread apart. Martin stood next to the bed and was fucking her in the vagina, which was right at the edge of the bed. His hands grabbed her around the hips and kept her in place. In Ellen's absence, Martin had removed all the bedclothes from the bed except for a white cotton sheet and a woolen blanket. The blanket was tangled up in Jane's twisted, clutching arms and was making her sweat, not uncharmingly. But Martin's jaw was clenched and his eyes were shut. He was working the vectors.

In order to have sex with Ellen, and turn this unholy act into simple premarital sex, he had only to position himself so that the path was clear. Martin knew that Ellen was being held captive in a Holiday Inn in Louisville, Kentucky. The hotel was near to a shopping mall and several clubs. Having been there himself, he was quite sure of her position in the room and the angle of her body. She had been tied up with rope at her wrists and ankles, and a piece of duct tape was firmly attached to her mouth. The skin around her mouth was kind of raw and disgusting from having the duct tape removed and reapplied, but her face was relaxed and peaceful because she was thinking about having sex with him. This was what made it so perfect.

With the thrust of his hips providing an engine, Martin steered the prostrate form of Jane down south over Ohio. Her body was stiff in front of him like a giant projection of his own penis, and her head broke a path through the landscape for them, each thrust driving them closer to Ellen's waiting lap. As they reached Columbus he began to drive them faster and faster until at Lexington the turn to the right was sharp and scary. From there, minimal adjustments were necessary and the shot to Louisville was straight and quick. Arriving at the Holiday Inn, Martin was forced to hesitate, and trembled there at the threshold of the room, waiting, panting, until Jane raised up her valiant head and urged him on, and they flew into Ellen right on time.

Chapter Twelve

If Jane had been a real cop, she would have been more spunky, probably. Also, she wouldn't have been sleeping with Martin and she wouldn't have been hanging out with him so much on a casual level either. She would have really filed reports and she would have done other cop things like fill out forms, answer phones, drive a cop vehicle. But she was not a cop, not really. On the night she met Martin, she had been standing around in the police station in her cop uniform which she had bought, like she often did on a busy night, staring at the bloody victims and the bloody perpetrators, listening to people cry, and yell, and deliberate. The police had gotten used to her and sometimes even joked around with her. The police liked admiration, she thought. It made them feel happy that this little woman wanted to stand around, posturing at the front desk, leaning on the drinking fountain, yearning to be one of them. No one yelled at her for impersonating an officer. No one wondered why on that particular night she left with the spooky guy in the long coat who had been asking about his missing girlfriend. It was a busy night, and no one cared. Martin was the first person in the world who really thought she was a cop, which drove her mad with joy.

For Jane, life was like a fist fight between good and evil, with evil wearing brass knuckles, and good getting beaten into paste. Of course, if there was a fist and a face, then evil was the fist and good was the face. It was just obvious for many reasons. Violence was bad, and people who did violence were bad. Quiet peacefulness was good, and people who did quiet peaceful things were good. Any crushing was bad, so anyone being crushed was good. Any raping was bad, so anyone getting raped was good. There was never a saint who went around killing and maiming. No, saints were the ones getting killed and maimed, because their goodness drew it like a magnet.

Jane's favorite story in the Bible was the story of Stephen, who was stoned to death for reasons she could not accurately remember. What she did remember was the image, in her mother's giant bible reproduced in a careful sketch. The man, Stephen, clothed in a white robe and bathed in a cone of yellow light from a small open spot in the clouds, was surrounded by dirty, nasty men with stones in their hands. Stephen was obviously near to death, although no wounds were visible, because he clutched at his chest with one hand and reached upwards with his other. His face, a vision of purity, lifted toward the source of the light, so girlish in its smoothness, every hair in place.

She had carried this image with her to the playground at her parochial school, where her enforced recreation of the scene was so realistic that she herself at one point actually fainted and had a knob on her head for days, which she feverishly touched at night in bed. When she got Barbies, they were martyr Barbies, straight out of Fox's book. Homemade instruments. Tableaux under the bed. She made her brother burn her at the stake, turned her dog into a ferocious lion, and gave herself a black eye on the bathroom sink so that she could walk around for days not telling anyone, preferring not to speak about it, getting weepy, until her father nearly exploded. Had he exploded, had he cracked her collarbone and split her lip, it might have been better for Jane. As it was, she was a martyr in need of a tyrant, a victim in need of a victimizer, lost in neutrality as she thought.

Until her attention turned to the police. Once, when visiting an interesting friend in a seedy neighborhood, she'd seen policemen drop a man to the ground, and stand on his head. The man was obviously bad. He was swearing. The policemen were obviously good. They were policemen. So there was a different situation, outside of and in contradiction to the one she had always imagined. Which is why she had to have the Cop Barbie as soon as it came out.

Jane had a lot of Barbies.

Jane stood her Ken doll precariously on the grocery store sign which she had made out of a paper towel tube and a box of macaroni and cheese. It was a high sign, with the kitchen floor of her apartment beneath it. She put Ken's hands right up to the top, high as he could stretch them, and Ken was pretending to be dying. Ken bent over and touched his toes, leaning his head out far, as far as he could go without topping, his butt leaned backwards over the side, in a suicidal triangle. Ken was thinking about how he wanted to commit suicide, just as Martin, if he were on the grocery store sign, would be thinking about how he wanted to commit suicide. She had seen him up there, on several occasions. She made her Ken doll think about how he wanted to commit suicide because of all the wrongs that had been done him.

"My girlfriend has run away! Forever!" she said in a deep voice. "With my only car! And I am sad, sad, sad from the miserable abandonment that I feel!"

Jane stood up, put her hands on her hips, and chewed her gum, leaving Ken balanced on the sign. Her kitchen was small, with a black and white tile floor and white appliances. If this had been the parking lot of the grocery store, then people would be looking up at Ken and thinking that this man must have been through an awful lot to be contemplating such a dreadful end. She sighed and raised her hand to them, looking wan and weak, and then dropped it back down to her side again, letting both arms dangle limply as her head nodded sagely in response. She waited patiently. And then raised her toe and nudged Ken in the butt so that he fell down off the sign and hit his head on the tile and landed on his side, still bent, poor Ken.

The immediate problem was that she didn't have a gun. She had never needed a real one, since she had never taken the cop impersonation so seriously before. First it was Halloween, then it was at home alone in her apartment, marching around in cop shoes yelling, "DROP IT NOW OR I'LL SHOOT" and waving a plastic starting gun that said, "Yahoo!!!" in bubble letters when you popped the flag out. No one had ever thought she was a real cop before Martin, but he never questioned it. In a breathless, mindless rush she had let the situation take her over, until she was saying, "I have been assigned to your case," and "I have been promoted to detective," and "I am driving a plain car because I am a detective, but here is my flashing light." Now, she did need a gun, because at any moment someone would ask her to see it, or she would be caught in a situation which required her to use it, or some other terrible thing would happen and it would just be better if she had a gun. Already when she had taken off her fake shoulder holster and slung it onto Martin's couch, she had had to fake how heavy it was, and cover it up with her jacket right away to prevent any investigation.

She could get a gun from an ex-boyfriend, but it wouldn't be a cop gun, and he would probably roar at her. So she would have to just go down to the police station and steal one. When she was little, her mother drove a banana yellow Barracuda, and kept a little shiny pistol in the glove compartment, all unloaded and pearl handled. Jane had been able to pretend-load this gun in ten seconds flat, and have it pretend-loaded, cocked, and pointed at her own little temple before her mother could veer wildly around, shriek, and slap it out of her hand. So she knew what guns were about. She knew the trigger was small and stiff. She had no delusions.

Jane sauntered into the police station in her usual garb and received nods from several officers who were milling around, and she knew all of these people, and these people knew her. She carried a couple of pie boxes: blueberry, and chocolate cream, with plates and plastic forks. She went straight to the stairs and tripped up to the second floor where there was a lounge with green vinyl sofas with metal arms, a wide counter with an industrial coffee pot on it, and there she set the pies down and opened the boxes. After cleaning up the lounge a bit, tossing out used Styrofoam cups and emptying the small garbage can into one in the hall, she sat down on one of the slippery sofas and began to read a newspaper she found there. She sat with her legs splayed, like they did, her elbows propped on her hip bones, and read, attempting to look lazy and in-significant.

A detective she knew walked in, nodding to her and saying, "Heya Janey, I heard you brought us a pie."

"Right over there," she said, nodding to the counter.

The man cut himself a nice slice of pie and sat down at a round table to eat it.

"So, you catch any bad guys today Janey?" he said comfortably, mouth full of pie and wide face relaxed and smooth.

"No," she said, putting aside her paper, "I didn't manage to catch any bad guys. I think it's my gun. What do you think?"

She pulled the funny gun out of its holster and handed it over, and the man took it with a smile.

"I never knew you carried a weapon," he said with mock severity, and then burst into loud laughs as he pulled the trigger and made the flag come out, "You mean those stupid criminals aren't paying attention to this fine piece?"

Jane shook her head.

"Hey Bobby," the detective called into the hall, "Come in here a sec."

He showed his friend her gun and she smiled and laughed with them, finding it so funny, and then she said, "Hey can I see yours?"

The detective sobered, and then pulled out his gun and handed it to her, saying, "Now don't you go pulling any triggers, Janey, okay? Just look at it."

She gave him a dry look and flipped the gun over in her hand, expertly, knocking the barrel out and finding that it was loaded. She didn't point it and didn't cock it, didn't touch the trigger. She handled it nonchalantly as the men were taking turns pointing her toy gun at each other and saying, "Yahoo! I'm a dead man!"

Just then, as if she had planned it, an older officer came in, one that found her regular presence irritating, one who wouldn't find horseplay with a fake gun particularly entertaining. He grunted at the pie on the counter, and the young detective whose gun she had immediately engaged him in a conversation about something she didn't fully understand, some bit of evidence and the district attorney's benevolence. She shrugged a tiny shrug and got up slowly, meandering toward the door, making it obvious that she didn't want to disturb them with her presence. Later she could say she forgot. She forgot the guns were switched. She meant to bring it back but she had a doctor's appointment. She kept it safe. She didn't realize. She didn't know.

"Jane," said the detective as she slunk out the door, "Hold up."

He came after her and hustled her out into the hall away from the older man.

"What?" she said.

"Did you forget you had my gun?" he said, trusting, half-laughing, thrusting her toy back into her hand and taking the heavy weapon back from where she had holstered it.

"Oh," she said, "I was just staying out of Orberton's way. I was going to come right back."

"Well, you shouldn't be walking around with this thing," he said kindly, looking fondly on her and touching her shoulder for a minute. These cops, these things she loved so dearly, were all in love with her as well, she knew. Even Orberton with his old head and his grouchy disposition. They all loved her as she loved them because they were all in the same enigma. The righteous violence was a cement between them. It hurt, but it was good.

"I'm going to go," she said. "I'll see you around tomorrow night probably."

"Okay, Janey, you take care now."

"Sure."

In her living room, Jane dressed up Barbie in Ellen's clothes and made Ken drive her to the 7-Eleven, which was made out of a box of Tide laundry detergent, and leave her in the pink Corvette with the engine running and the driver's side window down. She made Ken go inside, shut him in the box on the white powder so that he could not press his plastic face up against the glass and keep tabs on her. "I'll be fine," Barbie said. "What if the man comes back?" said Ken. "What if you get kidnapped too?" "Never mind," Barbie said, "I will be fine."

If Barbie sat in the car and no one came and no one took her away then maybe Ken would finally believe that he was the real victim here and that Ellen was gone of her own free will. Or if she was kidnapped, then that would show something too. Ken looked dubious. Barbie said that if the man came back, she could catch him, which was what she was supposed to be doing, because she was a real police officer. "I know what I am doing," she told him. She had a police badge in her wallet, but it was from the city of Philadelphia.

The clothes fit perfectly. She'd chosen a pair of faded jeans and a long white shirt. Barbie tried to sit like Ellen would have been sitting, with her knees shoved up against the dashboard, so that her neck was bent and crushed against the seat, and her back was almost flat, but she ended up just poking her legs straight down in the leg hole like always, with her back not really touching the car seat, her arms stiffly out front. The car's motor idled, but silently, smoothly, like a good fast car should run. Jane turned on the radio so there would be music, because Martin had said the radio was on. And then she closed her eyes.

Either Martin was the victim or Ellen was. If Martin/Ken was the victim, then Jane/Barbie was in no real danger from a kidnapper, unless Ellen was the victim of Martin, in which case Jane/Barbie was in no danger, except from Martin/Ken. And danger was fine, and preferable. Danger was, in fact, looked for and sought after. It was the whole point. If Martin/Ken was a rapist, a systematic choker and rapist, author of countless brutal acts against his girlfriend Ellen, and if Ellen had escaped, run off away from the danger, then it was fine, because Jane/Barbie would not escape and would not run off, and the danger would come to her, and she would probably die of it, and in that moment of death, impaled on his blasphemous cock, she would look up into the sky, and see the cone of light. Ellen had not been good enough to be killed by Martin's raping cock. She had slipped out in a moment of wickedness, turned tail, and run from it. Well Jane would not run.

If, however, Martin was the victim, then Ellen had sat in this seat exactly as Barbie sat, and Ellen had had evil thoughts. Ellen had thought, sitting here in these jeans (or not these exact ones but big ones that looked exactly like these and with her knees bent and probably her neck too), that Martin was stupid and boring and that she, Ellen, would show him and put him in his place and leave him and ruin him and make him crushed and sorry and sad forever. So she had ruthlessly slid into the driver's seat, cruelly put the car into gear, wickedly driven out of the parking lot, and gleefully shot off down the freeway, crushing Martin into a sad, good mess, unsightly to look at, but sweet, an abandoned lover.

Or, perhaps, they were both victims. Victims of a man so evil that he would come into a 7-Eleven parking lot, jump into a stranger's car, and drive away with that stranger's girlfriend, subjecting her to terror and pain beyond imagining, before he killed her and left her body in a swamp. If that was true, as Jane so deeply and dreadfully hoped, then at this moment he was watching Barbie, as Jane feigned sleep. He was standing in a shadow somewhere and contemplating her as she lay there in Ellen's clothes, in Martin's car, the same car and the same clothes (almost!) that Ellen had been wearing on that night when he began his evil act. No doubt Ellen had escaped from him too, finding it impossible to assume that final dignity of tragic death, slinking away to crawl back through gutters to safety, marred but unscarred—the sign of a flawed character. Only Stephen could be truly stoned. Other people managed to keep breathing.

The man would jump into the pink Corvette out of breath with all his evil. He would slam one arm across her throat and with the other would shift and drive and roll up the window and pummel her in the stomach. She would see blood in her eyes. She would be unable to breathe. They would be peeling down the street at a terrifying speed, and Martin would come jumping out of the box of Tide laundry detergent to watch them drive away and he would moan and cry and be forsaken. In her choked and anxious state she would fumble for her gun, and she would get it out of the holster, and he wouldn't see her because he would be driving, and she would try to see it in her hands, and they would hit a bump and whoop there it would go right out the window, and all her hope would be gone. She would not yield to hysteria. She would not beg and plead and cry. She would crush under his fists and be dragged out and killed and thrown into a ditch and he would tear away in the car showering her with gravel, all while she was still silent and small. And blood would come out her pink painted mouth while she was dying. A cop who holds her gun well and shoots and hits is a hero in her precinct, and may deserve to swagger around. But a dead cop is a modern martyr. She knew that it was true.

Eventually Ken came out of the 7-Eleven and got into the Corvette.

"Well," said Barbie, sitting up straight, "I told you it was true. She wasn't kidnapped, Martin. She left you on her own."

Jane snuck into the police station in the middle of the night, and the place was pretty busy still, which was fine. She walked around the halls very quietly,

escaping notice, blending in. She only knew that she
was going to keep on moving around until she saw what
she was thinking of as an Opportunity, whatever that
might be, to get herself a gun. Circling the stairwells
like a phantom, traipsing up and down the hallways
and in and out of bathrooms, the lobby, the bathrooms,
and back, she floated like a phantom, watching everything and waiting. Finally she saw what she could do.
Ahead of her, at a T in the hallway, a man was leaning
up against the corner of the T, his back to Jane who came
up toward the crossing. He was talking without anima-
tion about moving some hippie college students off the
steps of a bank downtown where they were camped in
blankets, sleeping in protest.

"Protest of what?" he was asking someone Jane
couldn't see. "Protest of banks?"

The other man laughed and said, "Yeah, Tent City.
Every year the same old hairy mess. Shoulda heard
them in the Plaza."

Jane thought that she might creep along beside
the wall, keeping her shoes very quiet, and listening
intently as the man kept talking. When she was directly
behind him she could wait until he was laughing hard,
and then slip the gun out of its holster with whisper
fingers, and replace it with her own. Of course, he
would notice it was gone later. Maybe he wouldn't
notice it was gone until he was racing down an alley
way, ready to shoot at a thief or a murderer. Then he
would have no weapon. Jane felt bad about that. However, maybe he would notice it later when he changed
his clothes, and would be too mortally embarrassed to
say anything to anyone but his captain. Maybe it would
get out, become a joke. Maybe the detective she had
tried the other night would find out, tell them it was
her. But if she had a gun, then she could be for real.
She could hunt down a kidnapper. She could die in
the line of duty. The man sighed at the end of a long
laugh and turned down the corridor toward her.

"Hey Janey," he said, "Catch any bad guys to-day?"

"Nope," she said.

In the end, she got a gun out of her father's bottom desk drawer. It was loaded and everything. It was a .38, which was not a cop gun. And not an automatic. But it went into the holster just fine. And then she had one.

Chapter Thirteen

Ellen was sick into the toilet. She had her right hand holding tight on the side of her head over her ear, and her left arm was laid across the toilet's mouth so she could lay her forehead down on it. Wearing one of those goddamned flannel nightgowns.

"I have an ear infection," she mourned into the toilet bowl, her face hovering above the coldness of the water. "Ouch."

The bathroom was cool and bright around her and outside the window gray light revealed trees in the yard. Folded towels, toothbrushes in their holders, shower curtain shut, and a dish of beaded bath salts all sat in their appointed places around Ellen who was sweaty and sick. Every time she heaved, she would heave three jerking times, and then a long real time that tried its hardest to bring up something, anything out of her stomach. But it was seven o'clock in the morning, and there wasn't anything in there to bring up. She pressed her finger into her head beside her hurting ear to try and relieve the pressure. She plugged her nose and blew air into her head to try and pop her ear but it didn't work. Every time she heaved into the toilet she thought her ear would rip apart. It was the most horrible thing and she couldn't think about anything else.

Slumped there over the toilet, one leg on each side, she heard Jay coming down the hallway from the bedroom. In the doorway, his dress shoes clicked on the bathroom tile.

"Ellen," he said, "What are you doing?"

"I'm sick."

She twisted her face up to look at him while her head still rested on her arm. Her hair, in a ponytail, straggled down her back. He wore a suit and his hair was still wet from the shower.

"Oh dear, well, I've got—"

Ellen interrupted him with another set of dry retches. Her upper body convulsed tiredly, going through the motions.

"Get out," she croaked. She had wanted to throw up in their bathroom attached to their room but he was in there. Now he was apparently going to be everywhere.

He stepped outside the door and she slammed it shut and began to cry.

"Are you alright?" he said through the door after a few seconds.

"No."

"Well should I come home at lunch? To check on you?"

She was done vomiting now and was just crying. She lay back on the floor and pressed her ear into the soft bath mat.

"No," she said, possibly inaudibly, possibly screaming, "No no no. You should stay home NOW and fix me up in bed with medicine and the remote and force me to drink chamomile tea even though it disgusts me and you should bring me magazines and kleenex and you should lie in the bed with me, and take the book out of my hand when I fall asleep. You should speak to the doctor quietly on the phone and when I say, 'My ear hurts,' you should say, 'I'm sorry,' but I can't even puke in front of you, so go to work." Ellen, saying this, made herself cry harder, and the pain in her ear was shocking.

"I'll call mother," said Jay, "and she'll send someone over."

"No," Ellen sobbed.

"Well Molly then. She can come over and take you to the doctor."

"No."

"Well, Ellen, what are you going to do?"

"I'm FINE," she slammed her hand against the door for emphasis and choking on mucous. "Just GO."

She knew from experience that being shut up in a bathroom was a position of power, even if you were lying on the floor wanting to die. Once she had broken the mirror in a bathroom at a party and cut her hand with Martin outside saying "Let me in." Eventually, if you really didn't want anyone coming in, if you didn't feel like throwing yourself bloodily into the arms of the person outside the door, then everyone had to go away. So she heard Jay going down the hall and down the stairs and out through the foyer to the front door and away. But she was still sick and had to do something about it. She might go deaf. And she had no car.

She sat up and pushed her hands back along the sides of her head, hating the feeling of little hair strings touching her face. She could call Martin. Martin would be angry. Calling Martin would be like calling Mom to come get her from camp because she had a bug bite. Calling Martin would be like spending a camping trip in a hotel because it was raining. Crouching on the floor in the bathroom of Jay's big house, clutching her ear at the end of a crying jag, Ellen knew that calling Martin was out of the question. She must persevere. She stood up, using the sink to help her. She looked into the mirror at her puffy eyes, her red chin, her wet face. The right side of her face, the side with the bad ear, looked weird, as if she couldn't move it, as if when she talked she had to keep that side still. She would be like one of those people it's hard to talk to because you have to spend the time staring at their face. One of those paralyzed people whose lips move strangely. She would be the youngest one ever to happen, and would go through life talking only through the left side of her face, because the right side couldn't feel anything.

She looked back into the eyes that were in the mirror and because of the pain in her ear she couldn't even imagine being one of those people. She couldn't imagine anything else than being red and puffy and standing here in bare feet in the bathroom of this house. It was quiet, here in the house. She tried to make herself talk to herself in the mirror, to move her mouth like a stroke victim, but she couldn't do it. Her mouth wouldn't obey orders and her throat wouldn't make sounds, when she was telling them what to do with words in her brain.

"Blah," she said, letting herself speak in the normal way, just with whatever unconscious nerve things make those decisions. It was loud. Her mouth moved on both sides. She began to worry that nothing would make the pain go away. It was a sincere worry that she had, unembellished with "and then, and then" but just a worry that she wouldn't stop hurting today.

She opened the bathroom door and went into the bedroom. She dressed herself in one of the pastel jogging suits Jay had bought her for lounging around the house. It was fleecy but with sort of nubbly fabric instead of fuzz on the inside. It hung differently from normal sweatpants and sweatshirts. It was supposed to make her feel richer. Putting on her shoes, she felt like just herself inside these clothes. She felt miserable. After washing her face and retying her ponytail, she went downstairs and out the front door.

On both sides of Jay's house, the suburban street stretched out in regularity under the spring sun. For a moment she thought she might look like a young wife stepping out for a morning run, about to do stretches and then float off down the sidewalk, but then she couldn't even think about how she looked or what she was because she had to do something about her ear. It was making her right eye feel funny, and making her jaw stiff. Deep down inside the ear itself, there was burning that went out into the bones of her head. She walked over to the neighbors' house. These were the neighbors she had spied on from her window in her first days at Jay's house. The landscaping neighbors, who she now knew had a very smart doctor for a daddy. She pushed the doorbell and heard the far-off gong.

She began to cry again, not because she felt like an orphaned waif, or because she felt like the Avon lady, or because she felt like a tax collector, but because she had a pain in her ear, and needed medicine. It was the worst pain ever, and shut her brain right down. The mother answered the doorbell in khaki pants and a white t-shirt, sweater pulled over her shoulders and hair brushed and coifed.

"Ellen," she gasped. "What's wrong?"

"I need help," Ellen said.

"Come in!" The woman pulled her inside and steered her toward the kitchen. The house inside looked just like Jay's house, except that the layout was different and the decorating was different. It was a familiar kind of strangeness.

"My ear hurts," she said to the woman. "I don't know what to do."

"Oh honey," the woman purred, "Sit down here at the table."

Ellen took a seat at the kitchen table. There were napkins in the centerpiece, and a salt and pepper shaker in the shape of daisies. From the table she could see the backyard and all the landscaping.

"Do you have any medicine?" Ellen asked.

"I'll do better than that," the woman said, smiling kindly. "I have a doctor! Fred is at home this morning, so he can have a look at you."

"Oh."

Ellen laid her head down on the table while the woman skittered off into another room. She looked at the kitchen, and all the pots and pans and little canisters of this and that. Ellen herself had been using pots and canisters such as these to prepare breakfast and dinner for Jay. With a cookbook open and her bottom lip bitten in her teeth, she had used potholders and serving spoons. She had made casserole and sprinkled spices. She even knew, through the haze of her earache, that her pots were better and her spices more varied. She certainly knew that her wallpaper was nicer and her kitchen was bigger. At the same time she felt like she'd walked off a movie set onto the real thing. Maybe this woman's spoons were scratched in the appropriate way. There was gum under her table. There were dog hairs under her sink. A complicated system to make things authentic. She was too distracted to take notes.

The doctor arrived and Ellen sat up.

"Well hello there, not feeling so hot are we?"

He sat comfortably in the chair next to Ellen and pulled her chair around to face him. His legs spread apart so she could scooch close, and he looked at her from over the top of some glasses. His hair was speckled gray, and he smelled like soap. A gray cardigan was half-buttoned over his blue cotton shirt. Ellen nodded sadly and the doctor lifted a lighted instrument to her ear so he could look inside.

"Let's look at the good one first," he said, taking a breath in before he put his eye to the black eyepiece, and then letting it out when he was done.

"Alright, now the offender," he said. He turned her head by moving her chin over, and took in another breath while he put the instrument in her bad ear.

"Ow," said Ellen, flinching away.

"Yep." He stood up and put his hand on top of her head, addressing his wife, "She's got an infection, and a fever too. I'll...uh...Sudafed and Amoxycillin. And Motrin. Alright?"

The mother handed him a pad of paper and he scribbled on it.

"Well she can't go home," she said. "She needs rest, and watching! Poor thing."

The woman came over and put her hand on Ellen's head where the doctor's had been, petting her hair and speaking soothingly. She knelt down next to Ellen.

"I'll go out and get your antibiotics," she said. "Everything else we have here. I'll tuck you up in Fred's study while I'm gone, and maybe you can get some sleep."

Within twenty minutes of taking the medicine Ellen felt better. She lay on a leather couch in Doctor Fred's basement study, tucked up in a quilt, feigning sleep. When the mother got back and gave her the antibiotics, she acted drowsy, comfortable, as if she could barely wake up enough to swallow the pills and roll over.

"She's asleep again," said the mother. "Fred, I can't believe her husband left her like that, so sick."

"She might have been asleep when he left," said the doctor, writing on papers and clickyclacking on a computer.

Ellen looked through her eyelashes at the father and mother. She tried to replace the mother's face with her face, and wondered if she could emulate that placid concern by poking her eyebrows together just that much, and making her mouth small around the edges. She would emulate it, but not for fifty years. Putting Jay's head over the doctor's head was easier, because the doctor was facing away. Would Jay emulate this brusque efficiency for fifty years, all the way until he was dead? Would he keep turning the covers down, climbing into bed, climbing out of bed and putting his watch back on, every single day for fifty years until they were both dead? Would she raise a child? Would she stay interested in homework long enough to get through twelve years of vicarious schooling? Would she pull into the same driveway, right next to this couple's driveway, over and over until a new car had to be purchased, and another, and another? And would the child even be real? It might not even be authentic.

The mother left the room, taking the trash basket with her, probably to empty it.

Ellen thought about growing up here or in the house next door and being the daughter of this father and lying on this couch as an object of proud proud love. Inside this place, after watching them from the outside for so many days, it was as if she had been adopted. As if she was the daughter of these two people, and had gone to Wellesley. She would be here taking a break from running a magazine, or defending criminals, or replacing hips. She would be resting on the couch after having a deeply intellectual conversation with Doctor Fred. She and Doctor Fred would have been discussing politics or literature, or postulating on the stock market, or reviewing an interesting article in a professional journal. Doctor Fred put his papers away and turned to the computer to write a long thing.

Of course, being adopted meant that she was not Doctor Fred's real child, and she was not. But if she were adopted, she would not know who her real father was, or how smart he was, or what kind of genes or potential diseases he may have given her. She would be completely in the dark about her own special heritage, influenced only by the good kind teachings of Doctor Fred. Maybe her real father was her father, and maybe he wasn't? Who knew, when you were adopted by Doctor Fred? You could be anyone. Ellen fidgeted, rolled away from the room and faced the back of the leather couch. To be adopted, by Doctor Fred or by Lawyer Joe or by Engineer Tom or by Writer Frank, she thought, would be the sweetest thing. But she could never be truly adopted, because she would always know who her father was, and always wonder how much of him was in her. Then, under the influence of Sudafed and reverie, Ellen fell asleep.

When Jay got home she was waiting for him on the stairs.

"This isn't working," she said as he set his briefcase down on the hall table, which also held a flower arrangement and a small bowl of decorative rocks. Good rocks and not cheap either, bought from a boutique and each one chosen individually. The bowl his mother had given him and it was clear but an expensive kind of clear, not just transparent but clear with a purpose, which was of course to show the rocks.

When Jay saw Ellen, when he was all the way inside and heard what she said and really saw her, he got a little shiver of panic, because she wasn't wearing makeup and she looked awful, as if she had been crying. Not that he expected, not really, not truly literally expected her to come wafting out of the kitchen wearing an apron and smelling of pot roast but why would someone sit on the stairs and just wait for their husband to get home, or boyfriend, or whatever he was?

"I brought you some medicine," he said, and produced a box of Tylenol PM from the pocket of his trench coat.

"I'm not having trouble sleeping," she said. "I've been sleeping all day. And I've seen Doctor Fred and I have medicine. But thanks."

Her voice had an edge to it that he didn't like. It upset him.

"Well, what is it then?" He put the Tylenol PM on top of his briefcase and hung his coat in the hall closet. With her on the stairs there was nowhere for him to sit so he just stood in the hallway there.

"It's just not working out. This husband and wife thing. This suburb thing. I mean, where are we going with this?"

"We're getting married in three weeks," he said, "and you know that."

"Yes but then what? Are we going to keep doing this forever and ever? Just keep on with the suppers and the television and all these conversations that we have?"

Jay felt the panic tighten in his stomach the way he felt it tighten when he took on his first long-term project at work, the suspicion that it couldn't last, that he couldn't keep bluffing and bullshitting. He felt it when he met with his first long-term client, a client that was going to stay on board for years and years in the future, who would weather expansion after expansion, upgrade after upgrade, and always be there expecting the same type of smile and rapport, throughout the centuries as telephones turned to video, and video turned to telepathy, and the world whizzed around. As long as the client continued to answer a "Hello" with a smile, and as long as the reports kept coming to him in blue speckled binders, why everything would flow smoothly through the eternal process, and finality would not intrude, not by error or by completion. But should the report come to him in a gray folder, or should the client say one day, "You know, Jay, I was thinking of moving the HQ to Brazil," then he would have to sit very still, and watch himself collapse.

"Do you not want to get married?" he asked her.

She frowned and plucked at the banister, kicking one foot against a step lower down. He shifted his weight from one foot to the other, and he knew that this superstructure which they both continually built, which they both continually maintained, could be exploded by one word from him, or her for that matter, and then they would be sitting in space, undefined and out of control. So it was important that she not be allowed to say, "I WANT TO GO HOME NOW," or "This is silly," or anything like that, and yet he had perversely asked her the very question that would open that possibility for her, for the stupid reason that he couldn't think of what else to say. Perhaps, simultaneously, he had opened the possibility that she would unwrinkle her brow, laugh and smile, that she would glaze over again and come hurling into his arms and they would have pot roast and coffee and a walk after dark. But she did not do this.

"Let's go on a killing spree and be arrested and jailed," she said, "or let's move to Montana and buy a cattle ranch and get windburn. Let's explore the sewers of Toledo and discover an alternate reality peopled with medieval assassins. Can't we do that, Jay? I don't really want to get married in Swanton. I could have gotten married in Toledo. Don't you see?"

Because he had not yet irrevocably decided that she should leave, because he was convinced of the power of inertia and swept by it and ruled by it, he did not say that no, they could not explore the sewers and the rest of it. She looked very earnest with her eyes full of tears and her hands clasped together between her knees. Her body was tense as if she was about to scream, and he thought she looked very concerned about what he would say next, and possibly really cared about what he wanted to do. He did not want everyone to find out it was all a hoax. He did not want her leaving there. He didn't want the inevitable conversation with his father in which nothing was explained and long silences forced him to count slats in the blinds.

"Maybe you could show me what you mean," he said.

"Alright." She got up and he saw she already had her coat next to her.

"Now?" he said, but really he couldn't imagine putting whatever this was off until later, going on into the house as if they weren't in flux, eating or answering the telephone while this obvious thing was between them and stopping them from behaving properly. So he put his coat back on and followed her out the door, where she instructed him to drive to the bookstore because they were going to steal a book.

On the way into the big store, Jay's stomach clutched and fluttered but Ellen was as gay and bright as she had ever been, hanging onto his arm and sparkling like she had on the night of the party, because she was acting, he knew this act. She chattered to him as they walked toward the back, still looking like hell from her illness but very animated. Her ponytail was perched up high and her cheeks were pink, probably from fever, maybe this whole thing was a feverish worry that would pass when she got better, which would be fine, but left the still worrisome fact that she was intent on experimenting in crime, and was holding onto his elbow. They passed the information desk, and went through mystery and science fiction and on, way back to religious reference books, where Ellen selected a book called *Angels A to Z* and began to leaf through it.

"I find this book especially interesting!" she said. He thought her eyes looked too bright like you would imagine a demented person's eyes looking, or one who is sick with a terrible life-threatening virus.

"What did the doctor say you had?"

She crouched down, next to the floor, letting go of him to do it, and as she crouched there ostensibly browsing the titles on the bottom shelf she stuffed the book into her jacket and clutched it with her elbow tight to her body, and then she stood back up.

"Perhaps another time!" she said, and pulled him toward the front of the store.

"There are detectors, by the entrance," he whispered urgently into her ear.

"Don't worry, I'm picking off the thingy."

Sure enough, her hand was inside her coat and she was working at something on the book with her fingers. Jay glanced nervously around the store as they all but raced for the exit, sure they looked the picture of guilt, sure the security guard would have them on the floor in an instant, and his reputation would be sullied, his wife put into an institution, because he would say that she was crazy. He could say that she was an imposter. Or anything, just to get out of that interrogation room with the miserable lights and all the questions.

Light classical music piped through the store and she was giggling as they fled, shedding a tiny scrap of white on the way past the new releases table, and pulling him out through the doors, where she started openly laughing. They were halfway to the car and she had taken the book out of her coat when they heard a voice calling after them.

"Hey!"

Jay stopped still and turned around. An employee on a cigarette break came hurrying toward them, tossing his butt into a row of bushes. Jay began to sweat and consider boldly dashing for the car. But Ellen was rigid beside him, her face now white and her hand clutching the book in plain view. The employee, a diminutive man with an uneven hairline and a shiny nose, caught up with them and stood there panting.

"What book is that?" he said.

"It's *Angels A to Z*" said Ellen.

"Oh god, I can't believe this—I saw you looking at it in the store, and I should have stopped you then," said the man.

"What can't you believe?" Jay asked.

"Well, I must apologize for the cashier. He is new, and he probably didn't know." The little man reached out his hand for the book and examined it, then nodded and smiled with chagrin, "This is the fourth edition, and the fifth one is out. It has a whole new section on Sumerian mythology, and lots of new entries based on research that's been done on old Christian texts too. You really should have it instead of this. I'm sorry he didn't catch it."

Jay looked at Ellen in complete disbelief, and saw that she too was wide-eyed and aghast. The little man pulled an actual handkerchief out of his pocket and wiped his mouth in kind of a disgusting way. Neither Jay nor Ellen said anything.

"I'll take you back in and give you the new one. It's a little more expensive but never mind."

The man turned and marched back toward the store with the book, and Jay and Ellen followed dreamily, traipsing quietly through the store after the employee, to receive their new book. Afterwards, Ellen was sullen in the car. She took the book out of its bag and threw it into the back seat.

"Stupid," she said.

"Look," said Jay, "I didn't like that. Not at all. I hated doing that."

He put emphasis on the word "hated" to bring emphasis to the point that the recent situation had really already clarified. That she was being ridiculous. That she had to stop it immediately. She just glared at him with a sneer that was sort of shocking. Jay drove them home and they ate spaghetti out of cans. Miserable.

Late that night, when Jay was asleep, Ellen crept downstairs and went into the kitchen to use the phone.

She wrapped the receiver in a thick dish towel and then took out some aluminum foil. Then she dialed the number of The Joyride. Martin answered.

"Listen to me," she said into the phone, gargling her voice down deep in her throat, and shaking the foil next to her mouth, "If you want to see your girlfriend again you had better bring fifty-thousand dollars to the address I give you, three weeks from tonight. No cops. No friends. Just you. Bring the money and the girl goes free. Come early and the girl dies."

"Who is this?" Martin asked, but Ellen just gave the address, enunciating clearly to be sure he got it right. Then she hung up.

She threw away the foil and folded the dish towel. She spent a while looking at the calendar, and went to bed.

Chapter Fourteen

MARTIN'S PRAYER

Help me do the things I should,
Like throw myself from grocery signs,
Find Ellen soon, treat her good,
Stop Jane from fucking with my mind.

Though I haven't served you well,
Father dear, I ask you please
Do not let me burn in hell
For blasphemy is a disease.

If you really do exist,
Forgive me for my mind's excursions.
Tell me that you aren't that pissed
About my vision and its versions.

If I am the anti-Christ
Let me do my duty well.
Bring me to my sacrifice,
But do not bring me down to hell.

If this is just deluded sass,
Have mercy on my sinner's soul.
These visions really bite my ass
And all this living takes its toll.

Martin sat in the Manitoba Tavern smoking a cigarette and ashing neatly into someone's abandoned beer.
Patronizing the Manitoba Tavern on a Wednesday night
was still a graceful act of kindness for him. It was the
fact that the thought required a "still" that gave him
pause. Maybe someday, he would be required to come
here, because it would be the best place to go on a
Wednesday. Maybe someday he would want to come
for the entertainment, because he would really enjoy
himself here, and the company and the music would be
so spectacular that people would say it was "not to be
missed." He imagined someday walking up to the door
of the Manitoba Tavern on a Wednesday night and being asked to pay a three dollar cover. The thought made
him tighten his shoelaces and sit up straight.

The Manitoba Tavern was a two-story white clap-
board building off a highway in Maumee, one of the
scalier suburbs, next to a stoplight and two or three
blocks from a railroad trestle. It had previously been
called "Pinky's" and had been strictly a bar with an
apartment upstairs, the kind of bar that had beer signs
in its windows and a Pepsi logo on its sign. Now the
upstairs had been revamped into a stage and dance
floor, and the Manitoba Tavern had begun having
bands in on weekdays. The Joyride, Martin's bar, was
the type of place where the graffiti on the bathroom

stalls was encouraged by a black marker hanging from a piece of tape, and often contained literary references and quotes. The Manitoba Tavern was the kind of place where the fights sometimes spilled out into the parking lot, a gravelly space between the building and the crossroads, not even contained by cement pylons or bricks. In Martin's parking lot there was an ATM. These facts, Martin felt, were the clear boundaries between his club and this one.

One of the local population, ball cap shoving his ears out to the sides, visiting the bar for a drink after work no doubt, shuffled over to the juke box and played a Pearl Jam song. He slumped back to the table he shared with a few other men, swinging his hips and raising his hands a little bit with the music. The front door opened and Martin saw an amplifier thrust into the room, followed by a duffel bag, followed by a man holding a guitar case. The door swung shut behind the man, who said a few words to the bouncer before letting his eyes dart around the room.

This was Matt Rich, a man famous for the story, told by his drummer usually, of when he came staggering down the street outside the club they were playing in Hamtramck, Michigan, saying "Hey, I met some guys who are going to score us some blow." "It wasn't blow, it was crack," the drummer would say, "and he wanted us to go back with these guys to their house! In fucking Hamtramck!" He was the lead singer for Ten Pin, the unofficial house band at The Joyride. Ten Pin played at The Joyride every Thursday night, and on the weekends they played in other cities, opening up for bands which Martin had brought to The Joyride to open up for them. He paid them five-hundred dollars a week, one thousand for holidays like New Year's Eve and Halloween. They had an enthusiastic following from Bowling Green, Perrysburg, University of Toledo, and even Findlay. The band had been together for three years, playing steady at The Joyride for two.

Martin took a long drink of water and waited for Matt to see him, his mind thick with rage that was also resignation. Finally, the boy's eyes met his, and he nodded with an eager dogged smile. Matt pushed the amp and other equipment behind the bouncer's stool and came over to where Martin was sitting at the bar.

"Hey man," said Matt.

"Hey," said Martin. His face was as blank as he could make it, and his voice as low, over the drone of Pearl Jam.

"Can I get a beer?" Matt called to the bartender, who nodded.

"Are you playing guitar now Matt?" Martin asked.

"No man," Matt laughed excessively, "That's Stenke's guitar!"

"Are you playing here tonight?" Martin asked flatly.

"Yeah, man," Matt nodded, his face suddenly serious and his brow furrowed and earnest. "Just as a special favor to Bob you know, he's starting up this night...this...on Wednesdays..."

"Battle of the Bands," Martin put in.

"Yeah, Battle of the Bands, and like...he wanted to get it started off with like something that people would want to shoot for, you know." Matt took a long swig of his beer, his curly hair falling back from his round face. Martin noted that he did not pay for the beer, nor was he asked to pay.

"Well," said Martin.

"Yeah," Matt nodded as if he understood himself perfectly, as if he was quite open to his point, as if he made good sense to himself. He looked smug, but then his eyes were always half-closed.

"If you play in this club tonight, you know you will not be playing my club tomorrow night, nor will you ever play in my club again," said Martin, as kindly as he might have said, "Blessed are the meek," if such a thing were required.

When Martin had bought The Joyride from its previous owner, that previous owner had given him a lecture. "In this town you've got a life expectancy of three years," the man had said. "What do you got here? You got college kids. You come on the scene, you're the new place, the frontier, and you get your regulars, your kids who like to explore shit, and you boom. Then your regulars graduate, move away, get knocked up, get jobs, whatever. You're left with a couple of fucking graduate students who don't buy anything but tonic water, and most of them want to come play guitar on a Tuesday and take home fifty bucks. This ain't your place for a nightclub to age. It ain't a retirement home for nightclubs." Martin had later planned on changing the name, hiring new waitresses, painting, growing a goatee, and coming back fresh. Then when the visions began, he had decided hey, what the fuck— grow a beard, some red paint on the palms and ankles, a short plummet into pavement and save the world. But in his first year of business, he actually thought he could force Toledo into being a place for living legends.

Martin climbed the stairs to the upper level and each step felt like a Herculean effort far beyond his power. He carried in his left hand a tall glass of water, in his right a smoldering cigarette, and he walked erect, balls of his feet landing on each step he climbed, turtleneck tight to his torso. The last vision had featured a cloud-break full of streaming light. The one before that transplanted the grocery store sign to a clean hilltop, wet with rain, green, ancient. He had seen himself in sandals, himself arms outstretched. Martin's head rose above the railing upstairs and he saw the darkness of the walls, the dirty floor, the decor that couldn't afford to be anything but black. And he thought that this is probably what the underground looks like. Tomblike, but an upstairs room. Maybe he could haul a truckload of dirt into his place and strew it around. Maybe he could hand out Clorox at the door along with convenient plastic cups, the kind you get at keggers, disposable. He wondered if he could even kill himself now, or if now he really had to kill himself. Either he couldn't, or he had to. It was a guess.

Faces rose to look at him as he walked through the gathering crowd to the back and sat down at a table lit by a small candle in a bowl. He smashed his cigarette butt into the light of the wick, and held it there in the cooling wax until it stayed erect on its own, a vulgar paper flame. There were no ashtrays in the place. Folding one leg over the other, he watched the four boys from Ten Pin having their little conference at the back of the stage. Their equipment was set up in the rear, with the two other bands that would be going first layered in front of it. Stenke, the guitar player and the only one of the bunch with any sense, though what he had was minimal, was grasping the top of a microphone with one hand and had the other hand on his hips. His head was dropped over and Martin saw him mouth the word "bastard." Martin smiled. Tough being a musician, thought Martin.

The sound system chugged out Echo and the Bunnymen and Martin could see the scruffy heads around him bobbing appreciatively. Really, the underground is here now, thought Martin without much distress. I am an antiseptic nightly news program and this is cable access. Lively. In 1989, even the frat boys dyed their hair yellow and black. Now, in 1990, nobody wants to shave. But it won't make money until you can sell tickets on rumors from the old days when people used to fuck in the bathroom. Then the girls in cardigans will swarm in and fuck lead singers in less exciting places, because no one ever fucked in the bathroom, not even in the old days, which would be now. Martin sighed through his teeth as the band approached him, now joined by the owner of this place, Bob, who had been a cook once. Looking at Bob made him feel like he'd just stepped in dog vomit when he wasn't wearing any shoes.

"Dude, man, this is so unfair," Matt began, slapping one palm with the backs of the fingers of his other hand. "Why can't we play tomorrow?"

"You can play tomorrow. But not if you play here tonight."

"Are you serious, man?" the drummer interjected. "Because come on we are not even getting paid tonight!"

Martin lit a cigarette and suppressed a smile.

"Yeah," said Stenke, explaining, "But that is not the point."

"What are you trying to do here?" Bob interjected, wiping his hands nervously on his pants. "What are you trying to pull?"

"Dude, don't do this again!" Matt whined, his eyes squeezed together. "You are like killing us here! We promised!"

Stenke's face was red and angry, but he hung back, resigned, perhaps ready to pack up and go. "You're killing Toledo, man," he said. "You may be surviving for now but you're killing yourself in the long run."

Martin looked at Stenke with his blankest expression. He consciously relaxed the muscles around his eyes and mouth so that not even his cigarette smoke could make him squint. Stenke was right, in a romantic sort of way. A prophet, but it was easy to do it.

"Should we pack up or what?" the bass player said to Stenke, scowling.

"No, man," said Matt, "We're playing here. We can do without this asshole, right Bob?"

Bob nodded and grinned, not looking into Martin's face.

"We need the money," said Stenke.

"Listen, dude, the winner of the Battle of the Bands is getting played on the radio, okay?" Matt continued.

His eyes were red and Martin knew he had been smoking a joint in the parking lot.

Martin imagined lining them up in a row in bright afternoon sunlight in the parking lot of the grocery store. Stenke, Matt, Bob, the drummer and bass player whose names he consistently forgot, and, for symmetry, every owner of every club who had threatened his business over the last four years. He would put them in a row, and behind them he would place every girl he had ever dated before Ellen, and the exact number of them would be the same. Behind this row he would place every version of himself that had ever existed before this version. The pink, sniffling, allergic child; the disobedient, unruly teenager; the scrubbed, faithful sailor; the drifter; the schemer. He would turn his back to all of these. On his right The Joyride would be empty of all the cardigan girls, all the drippy dick lead singers, all the loud waitresses— it would be clean and real light would come in through the windows. Then Ellen would come around the corner in front of him—worthy, tireless Ellen, with all her unsurprising revelations, and she would be at her best, in a long skirt, looking on him with simple, wonderfully dreary love. And as they came all into his field of vision—himself on the sign up high, glowing in white, feet shining, head encased in an immortal yellow, The Joyride empty and triumphant, and Ellen glowing—all those things behind him would evaporate and he would know they had although he wouldn't look. And then he would fall off the sign and die, sucked into the perfection of a truly perfect trinity, dead for its sanctity, killed for its immortality, resurrected in its eternal life. Long live Ellen and The Joyride. Long live Martin.

Later on Jane showed up as she had said she would. She said she liked showing up to places in plain clothes and asking for beer and getting served without an ID. She said she filed all this information for future reference. Martin saw the beer in her hand as she approached the table and hoped she wouldn't bust the Manitoba Tavern for serving underage drinkers. If he was going to take them out, he wanted to do it fairly.

Jane sat on his lap and shouted into his ear, hooking one arm around his neck. She always treated him carefully, as if he was going to break or smudge, where Ellen tossed his limbs around if it suited her, or scrubbed her fists through his hair, or pushed him out of chairs.

"This band sucks," she said. "Did he just say 'Smoking Celery Hoses'? or what?"

"Yes," said Martin, his lips brushing up against her ear in an effort to be heard without shouting. "The song is called 'Smoking Celery Hoses' and the only other lyrics are 'You' and 'Love me.'"

"Do they ever play at The Joyride?"

Martin shook his head. Jane watched the band for a while in silence, her hand tapping the back of Martin's shoulder absently. He shifted in his seat and motioned that she should get up so he could use the bathroom, but then when she sat down in the other chair he stayed at the table. She picked his cigarette butts out of the candle bowl one by one, wiping her hand on her jeans, and relit the candle after digging its wick free. It smoked and flickered around. In its glow her face looked like a statue in a Catholic church, lit by the candles of petitioners, shiny, chipped. While he was preparing to try and shout a conversation, he played a game of solitaire in his head, and didn't allow himself to start talking until the last card had been placed on its appropriate pile, one pile over each of the band members' heads.

"Someone called me about Ellen," said Martin.

"Who?" Jane shoved her chair over right up next to his and visibly strained to hear. She even shut her eyes. The band played a Replacements cover and Martin put his mouth directly over her ear without touching it.

"Someone called me about Ellen, about a ransom for Ellen!" he bellowed.

Jane frowned. "Why didn't you tell me?"

"I am telling you," he said.

She waited with her brow knitted up. Martin was always amazed at how directly her facial expressions reflected what was going on in her head. As if she were a stage actor.

"What did they say?" she finally shouted.

"The funny thing is," said Martin, "I think it was Ellen!"

"What??" cried Jane, accompanying her interjection with the appropriate shocked look.

"I think so but I'm not sure. What should I do?"

"What did she say," Jane repeated.

"Fifty-thousand dollars. The voice gave a Swanton address. I'm supposed to take it over there three weeks from Wednesday. Alone. No police."

"Oh no way," hollered Jane, shaking her head emphatically. Just then the music cut out at the end of a song and she continued in a lower voice, "You're not going by yourself."

"Well let's report it and see what your boss says to do."

"I'll report it, but I can tell you right now what he's going to say. He's going to say I go and you stay home. I'll take a…a plain car…and I'll just deal with it. Don't worry about it."

Martin took a moment to marvel at her bravery and initiative. She was, after all, barely five feet tall.

"If it's her making the call, it's a scam anyway. Like I've been saying this whole time."

"Oh," said Martin. "Well you should take Stef with you in any case, just to be safe."

"Are you kidding," she laughed, "I'll have police back-up—I don't need him. Anyway it's just going to be your ex-girlfriend standing there pretending to be brainwashed and hoping to get away with your cash. How much money do you have in the bank anyway?"

"Accessible? About fifty-thousand dollars."

"See?"

They turned to see Bob coming on the stage. Ten Pin had canceled their performance, they were informed. There would be a DJ in the sound booth for the rest of the night, they were told. Martin smiled. Apparently Stenke had gone home.

Chapter Fifteen

Ellen made the mascara wand come up exactly to her eye and then with small even strokes she covered the top of her eyelashes, and then the bottom. She put the wand into the tube and with three even strokes coated it. Switching the wand to her other hand she made it come up exactly to her eye and then with small even strokes she covered the top of her eyelashes, and then the bottom. She thought, I am moving with mechanical precision. She thought, Later, when they take me out of here, and they are making their reports to the evening news, they will say how I was not myself, how I had stiffened, how my smile was the sick leer of a shadow, how I kept repeating, "Lovely to see you" and "Of course I have been living here for several thousand years."

She put her hand over the center of the beautiful white bra they had bought her for today, and started to pant. "You mean it's not 1954?" she said to the mirror with wide dewy eyes, perfectly lined and powdered. Then, without her permission, her eye winked at her. And her face broke into a smile. No one is going to buy it, she thought. Well I will just have to faint. It was impossible to figure out exactly what would happen later in the day. No amount of postulating or hypothesizing could assure her that every contingency had been exhausted. The important thing was that she was the bride, and that later Martin would come and it would all be much more interesting.

Ellen sat in her room, preparing for her wedding day, and wondering what would be happening if her father and mother were there. Her mother would be cataloging every piece of furniture, every window drape, every small rug, by saying, "This is nice! Ooh, now this is nice!" She would wander around the room with a girl-in-the-secret-garden smile on her round face, demanding a response from Ellen on every new discovery. "This is nice! Hmm, Ellen? Isn't this nice?" "Yep, nice," Ellen would say, with increasing shortness, until her mother became wounded, and began asking her father for the nice confirmation instead. That's how it would go. Plus her mother would be wearing waffle pants and a dumb smock top, and would later change into some outfit with an irritating blazer.

If she had had a better mother, one that had an understanding of veils and flower arrangements, which Ellen did not have, then perhaps the last two weeks would not have been so much Jay's mother dragging her around and calling her a sweet girl through clenched teeth and telling her "posture please" through a big smile. Her own mother would have been strong but indulgent, proud of every little effort that Ellen made. "Um, butter-cream frosting?" Ellen would haltingly say, and her mother would say, "Oh, Ellen, good choice!" and probably they would go and have a hearty talk over some thick bean soup. Jay's mother would be having a bowl of thin tomato bisque at a nearby table.

Ellen put her dress in the middle of the floor with the skirt puffing up in little mounds on its own and the bodice falling down over the front. She stepped her white-stocking feet into the dress and pulled it up around her waist. It was a pretty nice dress, all rough silk, no beads or anything though. "Your wedding is in your living room," Jay's mother had said with a closed-mouth smile, "Let us not have ruffles, please." Ellen thought that the family probably assumed she was pregnant. They all wanted a wedding soon, at any rate, no waiting or planning while Ellen was living in that house. "Make an honest woman out of her!" Jay's father had said, slapping Jay on the shoulder blade, and then winking at Ellen as if being an honest woman wasn't that admirable of a trait after all.

If Ellen's father had been there, in that room with her at that moment, with her dress done up to the waist and her arms shoved through the sleeves, it is possible she might have asked him to zip her up, and he would have stood up and walked over to her and done it promptly and efficiently, without saying anything wise or coy, without fumbling the zipper or blushing or being boisterous or whatever. This was a good thing about her father, that he did not understand when to blush. However good he would have been at zipping things, there would have been an inevitable conversation between her father and Mr. Harrey, which honestly might not have gone badly at all. There may never have been a glaring moment where her father drooled into a napkin while Mr. Harrey made correct stock market predictions. That's what makes it so dangerous, Ellen thought. All these tiny little things, so that when you do notice, you fancy yourself a fucking detective, and you go whispering around the room. Ellen wondered whether, if she saw her father and he was not her father—and she did not know—if she would be able to piece everything together and come up with a conclusion like "slow" or "off" or whatever. Of if she did not know herself and she were to observe herself now, brushing her hair back and using clips to anchor it, fitting the silk flowered headpiece on the top of her skull—would she think "Hmm, something not right." Whatever her conclusions, she knew that she as an observer would not come up to herself, the observed, and inform herself of the facts. She would not approach the subject and say, for example, "You know, you seem a little retarded. Are you?"

Nobody would, because they assume you already know. And everyone is of course very very kind. Ellen fought her zipper up in the back and stepped into her white pumps, each one with a tiny silk flower on the toe, matching the ones on her headpiece. She looked at herself in the full-length mirror as if she were a friend that she'd disregarded all these years, and was just now looking at with all her attention. What would she notice, if this were the case? If she weren't constantly looking into mirrors and making faces at herself, would she have seen a change in herself since she had been living with Jay?

"You're a sight," said Molly from the doorway.

"So are you," Ellen shot back. Molly's little body had been tucked into a bridesmaid's dress so pink it put the posies to shame, or that is how the color had been described by the fitting room clerk at the bridal salon.

"Are you nervous?" Molly asked, "Do you need, like, a big fucking syringe full of drugs right now?"

"Nervous for what, to go down and stand in the living room and marry Jay? What's dangerous about that?"

"There's nothing dangerous about it," said Molly, sulking around the room and dragging her shoes across the carpet.

"This is what you **wanted** isn't it Molly?" Ellen glared at her, turning from the mirror.

"Yes," Molly said, "So go down and get married because it's what I wanted."

"And what Jay wants."

"Mmm hmmm," the girl concurred noncommittally, sniffing at Ellen's perfume bottle.

"Well it doesn't matter anyway, so what the fuck," Ellen muttered.

"What's that?"

"Nothing." For some reason, talking to Molly was different from talking to anyone else. Some sort of complicity had been forged on that afternoon with the handcuffs in the fast-food restaurant, and Ellen felt like on the one hand she would someday go to prison for Molly, and on the other hand, she wouldn't bother pretending to like a casserole, if Molly had slaved all day, even firing the crockery in which the thing was baked. She would just spit it out and say that it was shit, if it was.

"Well if you've got some second thoughts about it," Molly said, "then you'd better tell me now because they are almost ready to start down there."

"Now what do you think would make me have second thoughts?"

"I don't know."

"It wouldn't be the fact that I was kidnapped and forced to live in this house, would it? Or the manner in which Jay's proposal came to me, via his little sister in the guise of a philosophy on child development?"

"Shut up," said Molly. She threw herself on the bed and laid there moving her arms around, picking through the covers. Ellen stood tall next to the mirror still.

"Why do you think I'm doing this?"

"For the money," said Molly.

"You don't think for one second I might actually love him?"

"Not for one second," Molly lifted her chin and looked Ellen in the face.

"You did a shitty job on me," said Ellen. "Sloppy. I shouldn't even know my own name right now. I shouldn't be making decisions like this."

If she were brainwashed, if she had truly been brainwashed and made to believe that she was Cheryl or Beatrice or Noelle or Freda, or Emily, then what a strange surprise it would be when Martin came through the door that afternoon. She would be standing at the little makeshift altar by the grand piano, and she would be looking into the face of the minister as he said his sermon about everlasting love. She would honestly believe that Jay was her lover, and that she was going to live in this house, in this suburb, for the rest of her life. She would be considering, maybe, getting a job to pass the time, or when she should get pregnant, or maybe she would be thinking about what color to paint the bathroom. Perhaps she would be thinking about loving Jay, although what she could find to think about that was difficult to imagine.

Then Martin would come into the room, and in an instant her whole reality would begin to swirl and change as she remembered her real life, her other life, her whole separate other identity. Yes this would be a feeling worth experiencing. She would feel that pull out of herself, and instead of Cheryl she would be Ellen—one moment Cheryl and the next Ellen—a perfect transformation. And there her new life would be waiting, a blameless car trip home with Martin and there it would all be, and she, Ellen nee Cheryl, would be staring around herself, completely fresh. Who is this Ellen? she would be thinking. Does she have a family? Does she have any hopes and dreams? What an exciting chance to be only Ellen from now on, and never Cheryl again! In a way, this would still be true, even though her brainwashing had been utterly flubbed, even though she was most decidedly already Ellen, she would still stand there in a white dress with everything looming, and Martin would burst in, still, and take her away from it.

Ellen stood by the grand piano with one hand in Jay's hand and one hand holding the plastic stick in the middle of her bouquet. After sort of demanding that the extra money be spent on lily of the valley, she found them sickening, and held them down low, away from her face. In the living room, people were standing up, clustered around Ellen and Jay in no real order, but they were wearing tuxedos and formal gowns, and the flowers were just as nice as if everyone had been sitting down in pews in the way they should be.

"Marriage," the minister continued, "is like a car, and someone is always driving a car, so someone is always driving a marriage. On a long trip through life, drivers and passengers switch places, so in a marriage at times it will be Ellen and at times it will be Jay who is working harder to move the relationship along."

Ellen distractedly decided that that was the stupidest thing she'd ever heard, but Doctor Fred and his wife nodded and smiled beside a floor lamp, as if this was exactly what they had been about to say. These two were Ellen's sole invites; the rest of the group was composed of Mr. Harrey's business associates and one lone aunt, austere and near to the door. Ellen had to admit that Jay looked very handsome in his tuxedo, very tall, straight-lined, and looking at him was fun because she knew that he had nothing to do with her anymore, that this part of her life was almost over. As part of an oft-recounted memory, he would cut a fine profile.

"And so, let us never become discouraged, but always look to the next rest stop, or the next state line, where we shall take a restful nap while our partners take the wheel. Amen."

There was a rustle in the room as everyone enjoyed a post-sermon shift of legs and arms. It was time, Ellen knew, to move along to the vows. They had discussed the program and rehearsed it. They would have the vows and then they would move along into the dining room and eat the catering and then slowly people would begin to leave until there would be just Molly left and as she took off her dress and put on her street clothes she would laugh and laugh at Ellen, and pound Jay on the back and he would look bemused but proud and Ellen would be married.

The doorbell rang. The minister stopped talking. Ellen experienced a small shock of panic that she thought might cause her to faint. Doctor Fred said, "What in the sam hill?" and Jay's mother said, "Angela, get the door." So as the company waited, mid-moment, with vows unspoken and lips unkissed, the austere aunt stalked over to the door in her dove gray suit dress, dove grey pumps, and white gloves. In the foyer, her heels clicked ominously on the tile floor. Ellen let out all the air in her lungs.

Martin had come. He would come in, and with his military training he would assess the situation. He would see from the blank look she had even now installed upon her face that she was brainwashed beyond oblivion. He would set down the bag of money in the hall and he would say that she should come over and stand beside him and she automatically would respond. Maybe he would have his gun or he would threaten them all just by his mad assertiveness. She would look at all of them one last time with a sort of hurt affection, rapidly changing to reproach, and then she would slide out the door and into Martin's car, and the reverse brainwashing would begin. This is your bed, Ellen. Yes, your name is Ellen now. This is your psychiatrist. This is your car.

"Who is there?" called the aunt, perilously intimidating, and shot a look back at her sister, the mother of the groom, as if to say, Fear not, I will dispel this evil. A business associate cleared his throat. Molly rolled her eyes.

"Open up! Police!" the voice yelled, and the door shook from someone knocking on it hard. Ellen's teeth snapped together and she clutched at Jay. The aunt's arm shot out and opened the door with a snap and it swung into the foyer.

"Hello," said the aunt.

First, a hand came into the room, holding a gun, and then the elbow came in with a hand supporting it, and the arm swung around 180 degrees, and then a leg came in, and then a small woman in a police uniform popped into the doorway, glaring intently at the aunt, and then turning to stare at the wedding party in the living room.

"Ellen!" she barked. "Who here is Ellen! Ellen, identify yourself!"

Ellen nodded slowly, feeling frozen. The policewoman was tiny, fierce, her legs spread apart at shoulder width. Now she had both hands on the gun and it was pointed straight at Ellen. She could not believe, could not comprehend what had possessed Martin to send the police when it was clearly her voice on the phone, clearly a hoax, obviously a game. It made her angry that he would bring the police into the situation like this, taking control, turning the wheel so sharply to his way.

"My word," said Jay's father. "What's this all about? Now…"

"Ellen!" the little policewoman shouted. "You will walk over to me and you will stand behind me! The rest of you get your hands up NOW!"

Minister, business associates, parents, and hyperventilating aunt all raised their hands above their heads. Ellen took two shaky steps forward, glancing at the faces of Doctor Fred, of Jay's mother, and they were all shocked, as if she had suddenly become an entirely different story altogether. In that moment, she had to decide exactly what she would do, and she decided that fine, fine, fine, it was not that different from what she had planned, and as she was brainwashed, she would behave in a markedly brainwashed manner. She would have to figure out a way to get upstairs somehow and get all her clothes though.

"No," she shrieked. "You won't take him! He's done nothing wrong—I **wanted** to come I **wanted** to be here!"

Ellen hurled herself at Jane without knowing which limb she should grab or where she would land. Surely, a police officer would be able to subdue her in just a few seconds, and then she could lie panting on the floor, wild-eyed, devoted. She ran into the police-woman torso-first and, being taller, knocked her over. On all fours leaning over the little woman, whose gun hand was thrown out to the side and who appeared to be praying with eyes closed, Ellen paused for a moment, unsure how to be overcome, and felt herself being lifted off the policewoman, because of course Jay had come to stop her from getting into trouble.

"Ellen what are you doing?" said Jay, picking her up by her elbows from behind, but she managed to grab the front of the policewoman's shirt, and so lifting them both, he had to stop.

"Jay!" cried his father. "Leave her! What is going on!"

The policewoman opened her eyes and Ellen could see her bring the gun hand up in by her body, and point it up, and shut her eyes again, and the policewoman screamed, "Get off me! I am serious!" and the gun went off, and Jay fell backwards, because he had been shot. He fell down on his back and there was suddenly red around his stomach area, and his tuxedo shirt was torn by a bullet. Ellen, dropped, sat down hard on her butt with her legs caught underneath her by the skirt of her wedding gown. The policewoman let the gun fall out of her hand. Jay sort of gurgled in his throat but otherwise it was quiet, and everyone was standing still. In the wake of the gunshot, it seemed like they had all lost their nerve for participating in this suburban scene. No one wanted to attend a wedding like this one.

"Call the police," the policewoman whispered. "Call the police."

This request jolted the room into action.

"What the hell do you mean call the police!" hollered Jay's father, "You are the police!"

"Oh, Jay, Angela, he's been shot, oh Jay," his mother breathlessly crooned.

"Let me through, and let me see the boy," called Dr. Fred, pushing through the business associates to get to Jay.

Ellen sat on the floor still with her gown twisted around her legs. The policewoman hitched herself up on her elbows, her hand still clawed around the gun. Ellen saw her drag herself backwards until she hit the wall with her head and then she lay there, watching Jay's feet, which were flopped out, each to one side.

"Do something!" Ellen yelled at her, but the woman just shook her head. Ellen thought that really her father should have been here. He wouldn't have argued or fought. He would have called the police when she said to, and they would be on their way, and then he would have stood quietly until they arrived, and he would have done quiet things and good things until everything was over, and he wouldn't have been huffing around and making things worse, like everyone else in this room. He should have been here, she thought. Someone should have invited him, surprised her, so that when she came down the stairs, there were her parents ready to smile and nod at her wedding, but who would have done something like that? She would have had to call them herself, taken it on herself to organize that as she had organized all of it, arranged it, forced it, carried on with it, controlled it.

Ellen pushed herself up onto her knees and scooted across the floor, then let herself collapse again beside the policewoman, mired again in the folds of her gown. She jerked the radio off the woman's belt and flicked it on, propped on one elbow. Nothing. A child's toy, made of plastic with nothing inside. Her eyes met this woman's eyes and she saw the woman was afraid. Ellen knew for a fact, being that close to the action, that she hadn't meant to fire that gun. The woman smiled at Ellen, a little dry smile of resignation. Ellen clipped the radio back onto her belt.

"It's not your fault," said Ellen, "It's not your fault—it's my fault. It's all my fault."

Because it was her fault, when Jay was bleeding on the floor, and this little person was probably a killer, because she had put all of this together, for herself to live in, and now it was all her fault and ruined. It was all real. Everything that had happened was real and authentic. Every terrible thing.

"I'm sorry," she said. She pulled herself over to a chair where she could sit up. It was the most dramatic scene she had ever witnessed in her life. Dr. Fred was on the phone shouting instructions. Mr. and Mrs. Harrey were kneeling by their son, one with her hand in his hair, one with his hands in his own hair. Dr. Fred's wife knelt by the wounded torso, and with all the crowding Ellen couldn't see Jay's face at all. It was probably wan and drawn, because lots of blood had come out of the bullet hole, and more was coming out every minute.

One of the business associates had taken to interrogating the policewoman, who admitted that she was not really a police officer, admitted that she was there illegally, told him her name was Jane, and said cryptically, "I guess you will have to arrest me, and jail me, and put me in the hole."

Soon sirens sounded down the street and the whole mess of them parted for the EMTs coming for Jay and the police coming for Jane. Big men came and carried him out on a stretcher, with his parents still clutching on, and then they dragged Jane out, her shoes scraping, and all of the energy seemed to seep out the door with the criminal and the victim, and Ellen stayed sitting in her chair, waiting for someone to look at her so that she could start to cry. But she could hardly weep and say, "This was supposed to be my day," as if some birthday guest had smashed a layer cake, or as if a bridesmaid had given birth. There were dead people, and killers, and it was all her fault. The last of the guests to leave, an old vice-president from the company, came over to her where she sat doing her best to be forlorn without being self-absorbed.

"Are you alright, dear," he said benevolently, looking half-afraid that she would respond. But she only nodded, and he pushed off out the door, closing it behind him until she was alone. And maybe Jay really would die.

Maybe Jay would die and her job from now on would be to go into the graveyard and stand in the rain with a black suit and a black veil and a large umbrella shiny with water. She would stand there with small, smooth gloves in a little circle of moist air in the downpour, letting one big tear after another course down her face, and when she looked up into the face of some kind soul who had stopped to say "I'm sorry for your loss," her eyes would be brimming. They would think, How young to feel such grief, and they would walk away with a burden on their hearts, and the image seared into their brains of her in the rainstorm, but her as a blonde, her with plumper hips, her with nude-colored stockings and a hatpin anchoring her folded-up hair. Maybe some young knight would make it his particular purpose to bring light and joy to those deep sorrowful eyes of hers. With this thought, Ellen put her hands up onto her face and cried for a very long time.

She was jerked awake later by someone unlocking the door and coming into the house, and it was Stef.

"What are you doing," she said, jumping up hastily.

"Coming to see how you were." He stood in the foyer, arms crossed in front of him. He wore a hippie pullover with bobble ties at the neck, striped dark red and dark grey. It looked like canvas with nothing on underneath. Ellen realized it was getting dark out. She crossed to the stairs.

"I'm fine," she said. "I need to change my clothes, is all. Have you been to the hospital?"

"Mmm hmm," Stef stood rigidly by the door, as if he intended to stay standing there all night, with the door open a crack, his arms folded, on watch.

"Well, how is he," said Ellen, exasperated.

"Not dead," he said, terse and clipped.

"What a relief," said Ellen, moving her hand a short way up and down the bannister and attempting a giggle, "Rotten way to go you know, shot by a cop who's not even real."

"They arrested her, took her to jail, and put her in the hole," Stef said without laughing.

"Did you…know her?" she asked.

"Yes, but I always knew she wasn't a real cop."

"Oh yes, of course. Well…I've—"

"He's going to be pissing in a pipe and shitting in a bag," Stef went on, "and carting himself around in a wheelchair."

"That's terrible," said Ellen, wishing she could escape up the stairs, "But maybe Molly can—"

"Molly and me," he corrected her, "Molly and me. We'll move in here when the time comes."

"Good."

"Question is," he turned to face her, "Question is what're you going to do?"

"I'm going upstairs to change."

"Yeah, then what."

"Then I believe I'll call my father."

"Fine."

Lying across the bed in the room she had shared with Jay, she did not call her father. In fact she called Martin at their apartment.

"Martin," said the voice on the phone, and she was rocked back with the familiarity of his constant audible displeasure at having been called on the phone, as if he had just bitten into a rotten carrot, and a phone call on top of that was more than he could manage.

"Martin, it's me," she said.

"Where are you," his voice was suddenly urgent.

"It's alright. The...police that you sent...they got me out. I'm fine."

He was silent for a second, then, "Are you coming home, now?"

"Yes, right now, Martin."

"Should I come and get you?"

"Oh, no, I think Stef is going to drive me."

"Well then I'll meet you at the club."

"Martin, I love you."

"I love you too, Ellen."

And with that, Ellen packed up her beautiful clothes, and all her pretty new things, and left Swanton, never to return.

Chapter Sixteen

It was late at night, and Martin stood on top of the sign. Now that it was happening late at night, it became obvious to Martin that this is when it had to happen. At night, when The Joyride was full, but the people inside were invisible, when the line by the door had gone down to nothing and the bouncer had pulled his stool inside, when the band stood in the window stage, their backs to him, playing a third set. At night, there would be no cloud-break, and no wind to billow in his robes. At night the blaring ambulance would be part of the city noise, a noise you couldn't call pastoral. Secular people suicide at night. It's when the atheists make their statements.

He knew that Ellen was home, that Stef had dropped her off at home. He stood up there, so full of love for her that he could feel it reaching out of him and The Joyride like a point trying to be equidistant from them both, an angle trying to find its apex. He was so happy, in that moment, that it was all over, and that he would soon finish his life's work on a pure note of absolute fact, that he was smiling. It was not stressful at all for him in the end, because his trinity was so base, so sharp, so pleasantly mundane, that even with all the symbolism of two-thousand years of crucifixes hurling toward him, points down, he could only see himself as saving Ellen. He was a tall black figure up there smiling on the grocery store sign and then he saw her coming around the corner, walking from their apartment, and she was wearing some new dress, and walking a little faster than she normally did, standing a little straighter. She looked wonderful, perfect, just exactly that way forever.

"Ellen," he called, and as she looked up, he imagined her squinting up into the shadows of the sky where he stood, and he let himself lean forward until he was tipping, falling like he used to dive off the flight deck into the sea, only with his hands at his sides, and he landed on the cement, and broke his neck, and was dead.

Ellen started screaming for him to wait as soon as she saw him tipping, and she ran toward the sign screaming "Wait wait" while she was running, but he didn't wait, of course, and she got to the bottom of the sign when he was already fallen down and twisted and spoilt.

"Stef!" she screamed to the club, and fell down on her knees beside Martin's body, shaking it by the arm, and crying loud sharp hysterical shrieks. Stef came tearing out of the bar, skidded to a halt by her side, and stood looking with a frown. Ellen had pulled Martin's broken body up into her lap, and she looked like a statue. She looked like a saint.

"Stef," she entreated, "See this? I didn't even give him one little kiss, I could have given to him that one little kiss I wanted to, I meant to, I was going to just give him one little kiss when I saw him really easy like that just one little kiss even though I have been gone but I would just give him a little kiss, just one, and I didn't get to give him that one little kiss, Stef, no, not one little kiss, that I meant to give him, and planned to give him, he wouldn't wait for his kiss, he just didn't want that one little kiss I had—" Stef rapped her on the top of her head where it was bent over Martin and said, "You can kiss him. Maybe he ain't totally gone yet."

So Ellen leaned down and gave Martin one little kiss.

Jane spent quite a long time in a prison, because it was decided she was not insane, despite her huge collection of vintage Barbie dolls—she was just acting out, it was decided. This was fine with Jane, who soon amassed quite a little following in her cell block, which turned out to be full of sufferers and sinners, all in a simultaneous state of violence and victimization. Her group was called "The Strong Survive" and by worshipping police officers (and Joan of Arc) they gained favor with the guards, and were allowed to meet in the common room with the television off. After she was released, she continued her work with prisoners, and became quite famous for her artwork—a Barbie tableau of the prison affliction, complete with chains, horse whips, solitary boxes, and tin toilets. If you asked Jane whether she had suffered, she would take your hand and say that yes, she had.

Jay came home from the hospital eventually, with a catheter, and a wheelchair, and a headache. He returned joyfully to his natural habitat, in front of a computer screen, where he met and fell in love with a woman in Tokyo who called herself "Lapdance2000" and knew he was a paralyzed mess. He returned to his job programming for his father's company, and achieved huge successes pioneering streaming data software, which he then sold to a software firm, backstabbing his father and making himself a small fortune. Many people, Lapdance2000 included, said that the day he quit working for his father was the day he was born. He worked at home, of course, and was cared for by a personal nurse and by Molly and Stef.

Molly and Stef got married and lived together with Jay in the Swanton house, but had no children. They joked that their child was Jay, who required lots of attention in his handicapped state, but could not get out of his chair, and wanted to be confined to the basement most of the time anyway. Molly graduated from college and spent her life developing cyborg technologies that Jay might someday use to eventually walk and use his left arm. She wasn't very good at it, and none of her apparatuses actually worked, but they all had interesting names.

Stef became part-owner of The Joyride, because, you see, Ellen was the other part-owner. She did not lie down in the street and die, when Martin took his dive off the sign. She didn't even avail herself of her entirely justifiable right to cry in the graveyard in the rain; well, not more than once or twice. Instead she surprised everyone by stepping up to the bar and putting on an apron and running the place very successfully for several years. She had thought, hey, it'll be like I'm this indomitable widow with brains and guts and talent, and nothing can stop me from achieving my goal of running the bar. It'll be like I'm this widow who stands in her husband's place in the family business, and she gets rained on, and she gets beaten down, but she's determined, and she carries on because he would have wanted her to, and because it was his life's work, because she doesn't want to let him down. It'll be like I'm this person who has all this savvy, and all these ideas, and they just come burbling out of me, at all the right moments, until I am a legend in this city, how smart I am, and how successful.

And it not only was like that, it was that.